Fatal Marriage

By Alicia Rice

Printed in the United States of America

ISBN: 978-0-6151-6849-4

Note from author: This is a work of fiction. The story is not meant to represent any real persons, living or dead. The story is based on the Author's vivid imagination. Any similarity to any particular person or person's situation, place, or thing is merely a coincidence.

Note from the author…

It's incredible how things can change in eleven years; the person that I was in 1995 is entirely different than the woman I am in 2008. Seven years of marriage, two kids, a great job, and dreams coming true with being a published author have helped this particular project grow and blossom. I consider Fatal Marriage my baby, and when I received great feedback to expand on it, I took it all and ran with it. I hope you will not be disappointed.

I want to take this time to thank some important people in my life. First, I give reverence to God, thanking him for his blessings and giving me the gift of expressing my thoughts.

To Antrease: I am honored to call you "friend." We grew up together, laughed together, and fought together. Even when we lost contact, we picked up where we left off and never skipped a beat. Thank you for being real!

To Rachelle and Dionne: You two have demonstrated the true meaning of friendship. Both of you have continued to stand by me through good, bad, and indifferent times. If I ever need a shoulder to cry on, I know you two will be there. You've been my sounding board, my peace of mind, and my spiritual guides. Thank you for being real and sharing this season of life with me.

To my Divas, Tonya, Katina, Yulandra, and Sharon: Thank you for your feedback, support, good laughs, and encouragement. I miss all of you dearly and pray that our friendship continues.

To my dearest Versel: Our paths crossing in Cincinnati was fate. You have been a great contributor to this project as well. Words cannot express my gratitude and appreciation. This small dedication will have to do. May our paths cross again soon.

Introduction

Falling in love is one of the greatest feelings in the world. Losing the one you love is the most painful. With William gone, my heart is half empty. I am thankful for the memories, laughter, and my two beautiful reminders of the best days of my life. It was interesting how I met William. He was so charming, suave, calm, and confident. When he entered my life, it was during a time when I thought I'd never give my heart to another, let alone marry and start a family. I have no regrets. However, if I could turn back the hands of time, there's one part of my life that would have changed indeed. A time that was well before William came along, the time of Anthony Merrick. The trials that William and I had to face in our relationship were all on account of Anthony, a bad dating choice that I regret with all my being. This choice led to my beloved's death, as well as the death of the destroyer. As I sit in this chair, it's not easy for me to tell this story. It's filled with such joy and sadness. However, I want the world to know, in hopes that it will be a lesson to some and even a warning to others. I, Courtni Masterton, will tell you about the love and loss I have had to face.

Chapter One

It was a beautiful, sunny day in Long Beach, California. I was waking up from a good night's rest (and good night's lay). I looked over, and I saw my boyfriend, Anthony, putting on his clothes. While getting out of bed, I grabbed my robe and got out of bed. My attempt to kiss him good morning went unnoticed, as he seemed uninterested. There's been a great distance between us -- clear signs that the relationship is truly falling apart. But then again, I should have known better, considering how we met.

My best friend, Malova, threw a house party during the winter. Anthony was best friends with Malova's brother, Daidus. When Anthony approached me, I was hesitant because I knew how Daidus rolled: he was a straight ballin', hustlin', bad ass gangster. At the same time, I couldn't resist a bad boy, especially the way that Anthony looked. Before Malova gave the formal introduction, I was checking him out all night long. He stood in the corner with Daidus for the greater part of the night. His raven hair hung over his left eye. His muscular arms had Celtic tattoos all over them. His chest seemed firm – every curve was in its proper place. For a man who was supposed to be a thug, he was very beautiful in his looks. When he introduced himself to me for the first time, I got lost in his hazel green eyes. The final catch for me was his voice. Whenever he spoke, his voice was very compelling and distinctive. His articulation was erotic, even when cursing someone out. It was lust at first sight for me.

I expressed my concerns to Anthony about his lifestyle. As much as I was drawn to him like a magnet, I was not trying to be caught up in the thug life. He assured me that he was nothing like Daidus; he had just gotten out of the game and was trying to live right. After the party, we talked on the phone every day, went out every day, had great sex on the seventh date, and had pretty much been together ever since.

The beginning of the relationship was beautiful, but it started to go downhill from there.

Anthony started going to this club called The Whiz. He took me there a couple of times, but I really wasn't impressed. The drinks were watered down, the waitpersons had horrid attitudes, and they had a reefer room in the back. Anthony kept telling me that he was going to buy the place from the owner. From what I could tell, based on my last visit with him, the owner wasn't selling. Anthony has concocted various deals to persuade the owner. Their conversations always end the same – Anthony yelling and cursing at him, and a private phone call going out to someone else. As the deal continued to go sour, he made less time for me.

Even though he will lie about it to my face, I know he's back in the game. Anthony worked as a cook in a fancy restaurant here in town. His salary wasn't bad, but it wasn't enough to own that dang nightclub. Not trying to say that his credit is bad or anything, but I also know that a bank wouldn't just finance five million dollars off the jump. Being a business owner myself, I know how banks work. He comes home at 6 A.M. most of the time; he never answers his cell phone, and he only comes over when he wants some. What started so exquisite has been reduced to a one-way relationship. His needs are being fulfilled while I'm treated like the common booty call. It seems that I have fallen victim to the old cliché. Anthony did just enough to woo me (and I'm embarrassed to admit that he really didn't do much wooing), and now his true colors are apparent. I'm tired of being second in his life, but how do you approach a man with that demand when you have never been first?

Anthony continued to run around my house to get dressed. When does it end? I was thinking to myself. Do I accept this behavior, or do I demand change? The answer to that question, though obvious, was not going to come by easily, if not at all. Before he could run out the door, I grabbed him by the arm.

"Where are you running off to?" I asked.

"Baby, I gotta go make this run down at The Whiz," Anthony replied.

"At 8 A.M.? The club doesn't even open until 8 P.M."

"I know, but Shawn is going to meet down there with Bookie!"

"Shawn Deiter and Bookie Nole? Baby, I thought you stopped talking to them? That's what you told me." These men were Anthony's drug runners back in the day. I sat on the bed and crossed my arms.

"Woman, you are not my wife! I ain't gotta answer to your ass. You don't pay my bills!"

"You don't pay mine either, so you better talk to me with more respect!"

"You get what you give, and right now you are giving me too much attitude, Courtni."

"Like I wasn't giving it to you last night. Am I giving you too much attitude right now? You only respect me like you should when I'm straddling you!"

"And this is why I don't come around! You wonder why I don't want to spend time with you. All you are good for is to get some now and then. Quite frankly, you aren't even credible enough for that! My future wife will not be a nitpicking chick that questions my whereabouts like I'm a five-year-old kid!"

"I really am starting to question why I even put up with you! We've been together for three months, and lately you've been nonexistent in this relationship! You've been hanging out again with Daidus, hooking up with your drug buddies, having females slip you notes while we're at dinner – the list goes on and on. I am fed up with this. You need to tell me if you are with me or if you want to be without me."

"I'm leaving now, Courtni. I need to go and make my money."

"I want an answer, and I want it now!" I grabbed his arm as he tried to walk out the front door. Anthony turned around and raised his hand. He struck me with a force that knocked me to the floor. I started crying and held my eye. You'd think my face would be tough enough at this point, considering this was not the first time he placed his hands on me. Anthony grabbed my arms and slung me into the wall. Clinging to the wall, I wept -- wishing he would just beat me and get it over with. This is what I've been reduced to, and I don't like it.

"You always make me do this to you! Why?" he shouted.

"You always have a choice in everything you do. You choose to hit me. I don't make you do anything you don't want to."

"And yet you stick around and let me do it. Since you want to talk about choices, let's talk about you choosing to stay with me."

"You're right, but that choice is always subject to change."

"Yeah whatever, Courtni. You always pull that shit. It always ends the same though -- you call me telling me how much you love me and how you want to make it work, I say okay and come over for mediocre make up sex. Morning comes, and a new argument starts because you don't want me to leave. Sometimes we fight; sometimes I walk out the door to keep from damaging your pretty face."

"Well, I can make it easier for the both of us - as long as you answer my question truthfully. Are you back dealing drugs? If you are, then you can consider this relationship over."

"I am doing everything in my power to avoid going back. Look, that's why I am trying to buy this club; it's a legit business that I can make money off of. When I do, I'll be able to do more for you and spend more time with you. I love you and I don't want to lose you, but I gotta take care of my business, baby."

"You're like a broken record that repeats after the third verse. I'm getting to a point where your words don't mean shit to me anymore. Your mouth says one thing, but you do another. In the past two weeks, you have been treating me like a whore turning tricks for you. I am tired of it, Anthony. I am all about actions and your actions thus far had not shown that you care, love me, or whatever you're trying to get me to believe."

"I know, baby," Anthony backed away and grabbed his motorcycle helmet. Even though I was pouring out my heart as always, he refuses to listen. I keep wondering to myself, why do I even stay around this fool? He opened the door, "I just need to get this done. Things will be better once I get back on my game and make that paper. Just hold out a little longer."

"I can't keep waiting on you to do right by me, Anthony!"

"Just get yourself cleaned up and fix your eye. I'm sorry for hitting you. I'll holla' at you later baby."

He slammed the door and left. I sat on the floor, sobbing like I always do every time I see him. I got up and went to the bathroom, applying cold water to my eye. As I looked into the mirror at my caramel colored skin – offset by my black and blue eyes, I thought to myself, this has got to stop. My long, dainty black hair was a mess. Between the rough sex from the night before and the fresh slap across my face, I had tangles everywhere. I should be grateful. At least nothing else is bruised. Usually, I walk away from our fights with bruised arms, whip lashes on my curved backside, or bite marks on my neck or breast.

I had a photo shoot to do today, and I'm canceling it. The last time I did a shoot with a black eye, the client asked way too many questions. Their bodyguard even offered to beat up the person who did it. Right when I picked up the phone to make the call, it was Varsha already on the line.

"Dang girl, you picked the phone up quick," Varsha said. Varsha has been my friend since my family moved to Long Beach. She and her boyfriend were a part of my welcome committee to Long Beach in middle school.

"The phone was already in my hand anyway. I was about to call and cancel my Nora Kennedy shoot," I replied.

"Girl, are you crazy?!? That's NORA KENNEDY! You were supposed to get her autograph for me today."

"I know Varsha, and I am sorry. I'm just feeling a bit under the weather today. She's cool, people, and it's enough time for me to cancel the shoot and reschedule."

"Anthony must have just left, and he must have hit you again."

"Is it that obvious?"

"Girl, I think I'm used to it. What I am not used to is the fact that you have been keeping all of this from Malova. You know if Malova knew…"

"She would have him locked up -- but not before she beat his ass. Please continue to keep this secret for me."

"I'm trying my best, but she already wants him marked, and she doesn't even know what's going on. Malova is ready to go postal on the information that I found out about Anthony."

"What do you mean, Varsha?"

"I'm going to be honest with you, Courtni. I don't even want to tell you because I think no matter what, you won't leave him. You let this dude slap you around and stuff. That should be enough right there to leave him alone." I felt myself getting angry, even though I didn't have any right. Unfortunately, Varsha was correct. I wanted to shut her down and say, "Forget it," but I knew that wouldn't be beneficial. Something inside was telling me to calm down and listen to what she had to say.

"Okay, Varsha, it sounds like you have some knowledge to share; so just go on and tell me."

"I can do better than that if you like. You know how my detective/spy agency has been booming lately."

"Yeah, so what does it have to do with me?"

"Well, thanks for the encouragement..."

"I didn't mean it like that, sweetie. I'm sorry. Please continue with what you were saying."

"A client by the name of Joanne De Von came to see me last week. She wanted to know if her man was cheating on her, so she hired me to have him followed. Courtni, her man was Anthony."

"What!?!"

"Yeah, when she showed me the picture of them together in Las Vegas, I knew it was him. As a result, I told her that yeah, he was cheating -- in fact he was with you. I didn't give your name, but I told her he had been in a relationship with one of my best friends for about three months. She believed me, but she still hired me to follow him and have him tapped. I have him on tape with you and two other females. The footage I captured was more than just taking these various chicks out on dates. I also got footage on him having kinky sex with these women. I gave her a copy of the tape, his phone records and taped phone conversations. I kept copies to show you, if you don't believe me."

I could feel my heart leaving my body and smashing to the floor. Moreover, I thought I had to worry about him selling drugs and being a gangster. I started crying harder than before. I would have almost preferred the beatings versus finding out, he was cheating. At that moment, I had never felt so low. I've been played before but not like this. The tears escaping me fell to the floor in a crash. Even though I held the phone in my hand, I could no longer hear Varsha. Boom, boom -- the tears continued. I started hearing touch tones. That brought me back to reality long enough to finish my phone conversation.

"Varsha, I can't deal with this right now. I've got to go."

"I didn't tell you this to hurt you. I wasn't even going to tell you."

"You said that you saw him on tape with two other females, do you have names?"

"I do -- Adrienne Adams and Sarah Kelly. I can email you all the info if you want."

"Yeah, I do. I want to see it."

"You want me to come over?"

"Nope. I'm good. I need to get ready for that photo shoot. I'm tired of putting my life on hold for this boy. I'm going to reclaim my life! It starts right now!"

"I won't lie; I'm happy to hear that. I'm sorry that it took something so drastic for you to realize it."

"I put myself through all this unnecessary bullshit. I'm getting what I deserve, but it's cool. I know what I need to do. I'll holla at you later. Let me get over to this beach and get your long overdue autograph of Ms. Kennedy."

"Alright girl, I love you, Courtni. Remember that."

"I know you do, and I love you too. I'll talk to you later."

I hung up the phone and went to the bathroom. I was still tempted to cancel, but I cleaned up my face and went to work. I was actually glad I did because Ms. Kennedy's agent hired me to be the photographer in her upcoming wedding to Neil Hampton, the famous freelance artist. His drawings were very popular on the West Coast.

I dropped my bags and checked my messages. Anthony had called and said he wanted to talk to me about something extremely important. He wanted me to call him when I got home, but it wasn't happening. I jumped in the shower after listening to all my messages. The water felt so good upon my body and my soul. All of the stress, sorrow and pain seemed to have washed down the drain. All that were left was peace. After getting out of the shower, I put on my robe and went to my computer. I knew I could count on Varsha to deliver, and you better believe all the information was waiting for me in my AOL inbox. I looked at the phone records, pictures and watched two minutes of the video. I felt disconnected from the whole issue, as if I didn't even care about any of it. Right when I was about to compose a message to Varsha to say thank you, I heard the familiar tune of, "You got mail!" I saw it was an email from Anthony.

Baby, when you get this message, I need you to call me or IM me. I'll be on either from my house or on my cell.

I clicked the reply key on my screen. I attached all of the information that Varsha sent me in her email. I removed all her agency information because I didn't want him to go after her. They say you can never take the mentality out of a true gangster. So I didn't want to risk him going after her because she busted him.

You know, I found out some very interesting news today. Attached to this email are photos, video recordings of you with other women and your phone records to support the rest of the documentation. How could you do this to me? I put trust in our relationship! I'm going to do something that I should have done a long time ago. I need to have peace of mind. You can consider this relationship over! I don't want to hear from you -- ever! Anything that belongs to you in my house you can collect from the dumpster before Thursday, because that's trash day.

I sent the email off and attached a read receipt to it. I felt good about my decision, but I was still had a sense of sorrow. Why can't I find a guy that will be faithful? Every relationship I have ever had, the man always cheated! I don't understand it, and it's very frustrating. Maybe I should just get used to being alone. I think it's safer that way.

"You got mail!" sounded again. It was Anthony responding to my message. All the email said was, "Well there you have it. Bye then." I wanted to break down, but my pride wouldn't allow it. I kept telling myself if he doesn't care about what he did, why should I? It's time to move on and that chapter of my life has come to a close.

Chapter Two

It seemed like a desolate summer day in Long Beach, California. I was relaxing on the front porch thinking about my life and recent events. Breaking up with Anthony did a long time coming, but it still felt very strange know he wouldn't make his sorry calls or emails anymore and no more late night booty calls. Then again, no more good morning slaps across my face. At the end of the day, I had finally seen Anthony for who he truly was: a lack of a man that I had an unhealthy, whirlwind romance with, and it clearly ended in disaster. I wouldn't even call it a romance. Near the end I was treated like one of his tricks, and no woman in their right mind, or in this world for that matter, should ever be treated like that. In the beginning, he seemed to be everything that I wanted in a man. We were alike in many ways, but there were so many differences. Though it's pathetic that it took my girlfriend showing me some dirt on him to realize that it was time to be over, I'm thankful for it. The lies, secrets and deception on his part -- that is not a healthy relationship for anyone. For a moment, I felt bad about breaking up with him in an email, but I soon got over it. "Well there you have it. Bye then." Thinking about that response brings fury to my soul. It was a reminder that he didn't really care about me, and that all my friends were right. I found out the hard way, but at least I can honestly say I learned from the experience. While still lost in thoughts, the phone rang.

"Hello." I said.

"Hey Courtni, what's up girl?" It was my best friend Malova. This girl has been my rock, since we were four years old.

"Hey girl, what's shakin'?"

"Me, Mike, Varsha and Greg are going to the beach to hang out at the pier. Wanna come?"

"No, I don't think so."

"Why not? Come on, it's nice and warm."

"I'm already outside on the patio. Plus, I'm not up to going to the pier today."

"You're not still moping over Anthony, are you? Girl please, you did what you had to do. He wasn't a good fit for you and the entire world knows it. You should be glad that you got the upper hand first."

"First of all, how did you know about Anthony?"

"Girl, I was at my mom's house picking up some stuff and Daidus was there. He was on his cell phone with Anthony. He had it on speaker, so I heard the whole conversation. Be glad you did what you did, because he was going to break up with you."

"That muthafu--"

"Girl, he ain't even worth it, so don't go there. Now I will tell you he's worth swift kick in the butt! Why did you keep it from me?"

"Keep what?"

"After Daidus left to go and did a drug run with Anthony, I called Varsha and she told me how he had been beating on you and stuff. I figured that was going on because you were wearing your Versace shades way too much."

"I didn't want anyone to know. The only reason why Varsha knew was because she walked in on him throwing me across the room a couple of weeks back."

"Courtni Renee' Taylor, you are smarter than that. I can't believe you let that low life son of a bi--"

"Shut up, Malova! I don't need a lecture from you. This is why I didn't want to tell you in the first place. Heck, if you want to go off about something, remember you were the one who introduced me to him in the first place."

"Trust and believe that I regret it! I hope you know that if I really would have known that he was on that kind of level, there's no way I would have hooked you up with him."

"I know and I am sorry for jumping down your throat. I just feel like I'm scarred for life because I was so stupid for staying around as long as I did."

"You're not scarred for life. Time can heal all wounds. You only scar yourself if you allow yourself to make the same mistake again in the future."

"You don't have to worry about that."

"I know I don't. I know some of what I said may have come out the wrong way, and I'm sorry. The bottom line is I was trying to express that you didn't have to go through all that crap, and you know I would have made sure, he never laid a hand on you again."

"It's not your fault. I was being snippy. I'm just so damn angry, you know? I thought I had the right one that was going to be in my life forever, but it ended just as the rest of my relationships ended like a joke."

"Girl, be thankful. It would have been worse if you'd have married him."

"Are you sure that you guys are the only ones that are going to be hanging around? I just don't want to run into him right now. I don't think I can handle it."

"Well, besides the fact that it's a public beach, I don't think Anthony will be there. I heard he's gone out to Watson Island with my brother and the rest of his boys. Knowing them, they are planning a murder hit on someone. I heard Daidus and him talking about…"

"I don't even want to know. Just keep it to yourself. With regards to the beach, I'll go."

"Do you want me to come and pick you up?"

"No, I'll jump on the bike and meet you guys down there."

"You and that motorcycle -- girl, you're gonna get yourself killed one of these days. See you down there."

I wasn't really up for going, but you know how best friends can be. They think they know what's good for you. Actually, sometimes they do, but we all have our inaccurate moments. Besides, riding my 1995 Hyosung Rush always seems to cheer me up. I locked my front door, jumped on my bike, and was off to the beach. When I got there, the gang was waiting for me. Mike was Malova's boyfriend. Varsha and Greg are childhood sweethearts, and they plan on getting married around Christmas. I approached, only to walk up to Malova and Mike flirting with each other on the shore lines.

"You two can never keep your hands to yourselves, can you?" I asked sarcastically.

Mike's reply was, "When you're in love, it isn't possible."

I started frowning, feeling the bitterness rise inside me. "Please. The last thing I want to hear about is that four letter word."

"Oh Courtni, you'll find love again one day. Or better yet, love will find you." Malova said.

"At this point, I almost think I'm no longer capable of it." I said sourly.

"Girl, don't even claim that," Varsha started, "If you do, Anthony has won. You can't shut down on account of this."

"Yeah okay -- just want you to know that I am mad that you let the cat out of the bag about Anthony hitting on me."

"Don't be mad at her. She should have told me," Mike said. He came close to me and placed his hand on my shoulder, "I want you to promise me that if he or any man ever lays hands on you, you'll let one of us know. That don't make no sense, girl. Never let a man put his hands on you period! If he gets away with it a first time, damn sho' make sure he doesn't do it a second time. You'll hear I'm sorry, it'll never happen again, yada...yada...yada but they will keep on doing it until someone makes them stop."

"I feel you, Mike and thank you. I needed to hear that." He gave me a hug and walked back over to Varsha. "I'm sorry Varsha. I shouldn't be mad at you. I need to be thanking you right now. You saved me."

"Honey, you saved yourself. I just provided extra tools for you to make your escape." Varsha said.

We all started laughing and it felt so good. Behind me was masculine chatter, and it seemed like it was getting louder and louder. I turned and a group of guys were walking our way. One was fine -- so fine he made you want to slap his momma and tell God not to make another man as beautiful as he. His eyes were dark brown; his smile had a friendly nature; his body was to die for, perfectly chiseled. As he walked past my group, I managed to bring myself back to reality. I started thinking to myself, who am I kidding? I just got out of a relationship. Plus fifteen minutes ago, I made my anti-love comment. Besides, when I see someone as gorgeous as he is, I think of three things: taken a homosexual or a gigolo.

Malova snuck up behind me and whispered in my ear, "Courtni, there you go girl!"

"I don't think so," I replied, "I'm off the market, and I plan on keeping it that way for a while."

"There's nothing wrong with having a friend. You don't have to run off and get married. Who said he had to be yours for life? Haven't you ever heard of the term called friendship?"

Right when I was about to answer, Varsha and Greg came closer to where Malova, and I were standing.

"Hey ladies, what's with all the secrecy?" asked Greg.

"Nothing -- Malova is trying to recruit a new boyfriend for me already." I replied.

"Heck, I'm glad you're even out the house," said Varsha, "You've finally decided to join the land of living. You're out the house kicking it with your folks, and it seems like you're having a good time so far. You had a sista worried about you at first. I thought you weren't going to leave the house."

"Hey, it was my hard work and persuasion that got her to show." Malova said.

"Personally, I'm glad to see you up and around, Courtni." Greg said.

"Thanks." I replied.

"Besides, you can do a hell of a lot better than Anthony," Greg was saying, "forget him! He isn't shit, and when another man says that a man isn't shit, then that has to count for something. You know how we stick together sometimes."

"Greg is right," says Malova, "Anthony's a lost fool. You can mess up your own life without the help of others, girl. You don't need anyone else to drag you down. When you are really ready to date again, the next man should be your companion. A true companionship is a fellowship existing among two people who have a true connection. He will be your friend, be in your corner and stand for something. When that happens, you'll know; In addition, you will know that you two are a blessing to each other. In fact, that good looking guy over there that we were talking about earlier seems to fit the bill. I'm going over to talk to him for you."

"Malova, don't you dare!" I shouted.

"You forgot who you were talking to. Watch me!"

She ran over to the group of guys. I was so angry and nervous at the same time. The one that I was admiring glanced at me and smiled. The first thing I thought was Malova is so dead! However, the more she talked the more he started to smile. Then I started thinking to myself, maybe having just a friend wouldn't be as bad. I do know that's all I need for now and maybe even forever, but that's only if he's interested. I also couldn't get what Malova said out of my head. She ran back over to us waving her hands in the air and smiling.

"Here's the bio: His name is William Masterton," Malova was saying with a huge smile, "He's 22, single and just broke up with his girlfriend. He thinks that our Courtni, here is cute, pretty and some other mushy stuff that I will leave him to tell you himself. His phone number is 555-6790. He will be expecting your call. If you don't call him, I'm going to choke slam you."

"I can't believe you did that! What makes you think I wanted his number? Better yet, did you think I even wanted to know his name? I can't believe you put me on blast like that!" I was trying to pretend like I was mad. On the outside it looked convincing, but internally I was excited. He's in the same boat. He thinks I'm cute. Maybe we can be friends.

"Hey, all I'm trying to do is hook you up! It seems like both of you can use each other's company. Call him!"

"I'll think about it. If I do, it will be just one phone call and that's that! Nothing will happen beyond our conversation."

"You say that now, but soon you'll be under the spell of love."

"You can really calm all that noise down."

Everyone laughed at what happened. We all started walking on the beach, talking about what was going on in everyone's lives. We spent a nice bulk of it laughing at me due to Malova's bold move. At about 9 P.M., I stopped by Checkers for a hamburger. I went home, ate my dinner (or lack thereof), and curled up on my couch with my diary. It was always my outlet and my comfort when I needed. As I started to end my journal entry, I started thinking about William Masterton. Is he a fake? What's his story? Is he really a dream comes true? I guess one phone call won't shatter me for life, and maybe it will get my questions answered. I looked at my phone thinking, do I really want to do this? Do I really want to see what this guy was all about? I finally decided that I would never know unless I took a leap of faith. I took the number out of my pocket, picked up the phone and dialed.

"Hello," I said, "is William there?"

"You're speaking to him. Is this Courtni?" he asked. Man, his voice is so sexy.

"Yes, it is. How are you this evening?"

"Fine and you?"

"Fine, fine, thanks for asking. Look, I am so sorry that my friend came over to you and embarrassed us both."

"I'm glad she did. I was checking you out anyway. When you got off your motorcycle and took off your helmet, I thought to myself, now there's a lady who knows how to ride in style."

"You're a biker?"

"No but I admire anyone who's brave enough to hop on one of those things. I especially admire women who do it."

"It's not that big of a deal. It's just like riding a regular bicycle."

"Yeah but I wouldn't look as exemplary sitting on it as you do."

"My, you are a charmer."

"Call it what you want, but you were looking mighty smooth in your short denim shorts and that red tube top. Your energy was screaming, *I'm a sexy biker goddess.*"

"Oh, stop. You're just joking around."

"No, I'm not. I take my compliments very seriously. I guess I was a little nervous to make my move. I think you're beautiful and I'm just curious to know if the brains match the beauty. I'd like the chance to find out."

"Oh really?"

"Yes, really. I'd like to take you out sometime."

"When?"

"Let's give it a week or two. That'll give us some time to get some conversation going on the phone. You know, feel each other out a bit. By the time it's close to the date, we will both be certain if we want to meet personally. If you or both of us feel that it isn't worthwhile, then it's cool; we don't meet, but we can still keep in touch. Does that sound fair?"

"That's cool. I'd like that."

"Great! Well, look, I got some errands to run. Can I call you back tomorrow? I would say tonight, but I don't want to call your house too late."

"That's straight. Here's my number –"

I gave him my number, and we got off the phone. He sounds so sweet. I wonder if it's an act, or could he possibly be authentic? Who knows, he might be? I'm already feeling his style and approach. Despite my feelings on relationships, he has me interested in learning more about him. Lord knows I've been hurt too many times to go through more drama. I wasn't very sleepy, so I decided to flip through the TV channels. I saw a flash of Anthony's mug shot on the television. I flipped back and saw that his picture was on Fox News. I sat back in my chair to watch the news segment with anchorman George Whitfield reporting.

"Last night's deadly night club bombing on the pier in Long Beach is being called an act of revenge. The death toll from the attack at The Whiz is almost one hundred and twenty-five now. Fox News Brenda Hillsdale is on the scene now from The Whiz with the very latest."

"Well, George, it's been almost exactly twenty-four hours since The Whiz exploded in a fiery inferno. As you can see in the picture to the left of me, this is the suspect the police are looking for: Anthony Merrick. Police believe while weekenders were enjoying their time at the night club, there was some commotion in the back of the club and then a loud explosion. More than one hundred and twenty-five people have been confirmed dead. More than twenty-five are in critical condition with third degree burns."

"That is horrific, Brenda. Could you tell us all more about the suspect?"

"This suspect gives a whole new definition to a smooth criminal. From drug trafficking, attempted murder and Argo-terrorism, Anthony Merrick has done it all. Police sources stated that Merrick was to take over the night club from the previous owners."

"Were the owners among the casualties?"

"Yes, George, they were. According to the information I received from one of the surviving bartenders, Derrick Love and Shawn Deiter were in the process of selling the club to Merrick. Bookie Nole of the Long Beach Drug Cartel and Anthony Merrick discovered foul play in the business transaction. I'm reading here and it looks like it was over a woman by the name of Clair Vice. Now, at this time, it's all speculations. There's no real evidence that Merrick had anything to do with the bombing, but since there are eyewitnesses stating that he was in fact here, along with his criminal record, police want everyone to keep an eye out for him."

"Is he considered dangerous?"

"At this time, I will say yes. From a journalist's perspective, George, I would caution viewers to turn the other way and call police immediately if they see him. The fact that this notorious crime lord was here at the scene, police are sure he is the cause. They will continue searching for him, so they may bring him in for questioning."

"Thank you Brenda. Just one more question: If he's considered to be a notorious crime lord, why can he walk the streets?"

"When I called him a smooth criminal earlier George, I meant just that. Every time the police or the FBI has attempted to charge him with various crimes, the evidence or eyewitnesses always end up disappearing. The authorities never have anything concrete to hold him behind bars. Now, he has been arrested and charged with marijuana possession, but nothing major that would keep him locked up considerably."

"Thank you for the information. That was Brenda Hillsdale reporting"

I turned off the television. My mouth dropped to the floor. I was in complete shock. Seeing that news update just affirmed my decision for breaking up with Anthony. You think you know a person that you claim to be with, but what I just saw proved that theory to be wrong. Well, at least he's out of my life, and I can move forward. I'm actually anxious to see what this William fellow is all about. We'll see.

Chapter Three

William and I have been talking on the phone everyday for two weeks now. I was a little hesitant to even call him back after what I witnessed on television a few weeks back. Nevertheless, then I thought about something my mother always told me: Child, don't let the next man pay for the first man's sins. I never knew what she was talking about up to the present moment. God rest her soul, I miss Mama. Maybe if she were here she would have warned me to stay away from Anthony.

I made it a routine to call William after a long day at the studio. In two weeks time, I learned that he was from a well-to-do family in Mississippi. He's so humble and modest -- you never would have picked up on it. He's a Christian man (which is always a plus -- as long as it's not a front) and his philosophy is to put God first in everything. I have never talked to a man that speaks about the Lord as passionately as he does. He admits that he falls short, but he says he tries his best to walk with Christ and not be left behind.

It's Friday, during the second week, and we both decided that we wanted to meet tonight. It's been a considerable amount of time, since I've been on a first date. I'm not nervous. Yes I am. Why am I trying to fool myself here? Earlier that day I went to Macy's and bought a new dress. He's taking me to La Bonita, one of the finest Mexican restaurants in Long Beach. At 7 P.M., I was ready to go. Our reservations were for seven-thirty, so I wanted to make sure, I was ready in plenty of time, just in case he ran late. To my surprise, he arrived at my house at 7:01 P.M.

I had only seen La Bonita from the outside. The inside was an absolute dream and the food was excellent. While eating, I decided to strike up a conversation.

"This is really a nice place." I said.

"It's one of the finest in town, and I'm proud to say that my dad owns it." He says.

"Really? You didn't tell me that."

"I don't like to brag. My parents met in Lima, Peru. He was vacationing there and he saw my mom at one of the tourist booths. He said it was love at first sight. He spent so much money flying back and forth to visit her for about a year. On what they call their anniversary, the day he first met her, he proposed, and they got married. She moved back to Mississippi with him and six months later she became Nelli Izel Masterton. They've been together for twenty-five years, married for twenty-three."

"That's beautiful. You don't see that anymore."

"You're right. Most people, especially in our age group, do not know or care to understand the real value behind marriage. It starts with companionship."

"That's very true. My friend, Malova, mentioned that the day she came over and embarrassed us both."

"Really? She's seems to be a good friend. Those are rare as well."

"She is -- they all are. The group that I was with, we have all been friends for a long time. Malova and I grew up together in Alameda, California. Our parents worked together and we also lived on the same block. Both of our dads got promotions, and we moved here to Long Beach. In middle school, we met Varsha, Mike and Greg. Varsha and Greg have been together since they were kids. If they ever broke up, we never knew about it. During our 9th grade year, Mike finally admitted that he liked Malova, and they've been together off and on ever since."

"What do you mean by finally?"

"Mike was cool with Greg, so when we all started hanging out, Mike would follow Malova everywhere she went. He would have gone to the bathroom for her if he could. Whenever any of us would bring it to him to say something to Malova, he would say he only liked her as a friend. Of course, we all knew differently -- even Malova! She was just waiting on him to say something. She had too much pride to approach him."

"That is cute and funny."

"I think so. It's like a perfect love story in the making. Too bad none of my relationships was as happy as theirs."

"If that was the case, we wouldn't be sitting here together."

"You got a point."

"Besides, you may have your perfect love story sooner than you think."

"And why is that?"

"Well, for starters, I enjoy talking to you, and I am enjoying being around you. I do hope we can come here more often and hang out more. I think we are starting the perfect friendship."

"So far, you're heading in the right direction. You are definitely winning in the wooing department. Let me ask you, what's your history with women? A gorgeous, successful man such as you can date someone better than grungy old me."

"For starters, you are not grungy, and I am assuming you said that because you're a biker. Like I told you when we had our first conversation, you're a beautiful woman, and you really should stop doubting your worth. Getting back to your question, I was in a serious relationship with this girl. I was falling in love with her, but it was an one way street."

"I'm sorry to hear that. I've been down that road once, and it's a lonely one."

"It's okay. Things happen for a reason. The Lord showed me that she was not the one. "

"What happened?"

"Lots of things happened between Francis and me. She played a lot of mind games. When Francis wanted you to be there for her, you better be. When she didn't want to be bothered, you'd best stay out of her way and not ask questions. That's something I despise in people. Period. Second, I found out that she was sleeping with like twelve dudes behind my back. She got pregnant by one of them. And get this -- tried to pawn the kid off on me. How stupid can you be?"

"Um, not taking up for the girl, but why would that be stupid? Mind you, I'm not condoning her actions by any means, but you're a good man, and she was trying to keep you."

"I don't believe in sex before marriage, so there's no way the kid could be mine."

"Wow, that's amazing, but how would she even get that idea?"

"We went to a benefit dinner that the Mayor was throwing and we both had way too much wine. Luckily, for me that night I had a limo driver, so I didn't have to worry about driving home. There were a lot of kissing and heavy petting involved, but when I carried her to the bedroom, she fell fast asleep. I curled up next to her, but I didn't touch her at all. When we woke up the next day, all she knew was that we were both in the bed, and she had on her bra and panties. She assumed we did something. I think she knew good, and well we didn't."

"That's shady, but people can be like that. Back to you being a virgin, that just makes you even sexier than before."

"Thanks. That's how mom raised me. You don't give away the goods to just anyone that comes along. Anyway, as you can see, she damaged my heart pretty bad. I think of her from time to time. I think about the good times we had, but the bad stuff completely overpowers the good any day of the week. In fact, I pity her because the last I heard, she had the baby, found out which one was the daddy, but he's locked up down in Lompoc. Rumor has it, he got locked up on purpose to dodge the child support."

"That's foul! She's skanky, no disrespect, but that man going to jail to get out of his responsibilities is crazy and foul!"

"No offense taken. It was a learning experience for me. At least I can say I didn't walk away from the relationship empty handed."

"That is a good way to look at it."

"So now, I'm moving on. I moved up here to get away from her and to help my dad manage La Bonita. My dad is ill, so he wants to spend some time with my mom. If you have him tell it, he doesn't have that much longer to live. I think he's bluffing though. If you ever get to meet him, you'll find out that he's as tough as iron nails. He's not going to keel over yet."

"I'd like to meet your parents someday. Hey, I'm really sorry about all that stuff with Francis."

"It's alright. In the long run, it's her loss. So, enough about me, tell me about your past relationships."

"Ugh! The most recent is very painful. It starts with --"

As I was about to tell him about my ex, behold, he walked in...Anthony! The last time I laid eyes upon his face was while I was watching his mug shot on Fox Breaking News. It amazes me how he can just waltz in freely like everything is right with the world. He had a date with him. Not that I cared but, man, couldn't he have taken his date elsewhere? Furthermore, when we were together he never took me anywhere as nice as this. It was clear that he saved it for his broads that he got caught on tape with. I should be fortunate because one of those girls was murdered in the club bombing. A part of me was being a hater, but I was thankful at the same time. At least I can say that I was better looking than his date. I was praying to God he didn't see me. Why? Because, a normal person would go about their business or maybe speak, then go about their business. Oh no, not Anthony, he's the all time number one shit disturber. William noticed the look on my face and touched my arm.

"Courtni, what's wrong?" William said, with sincere concern in his voice.

"See that guy over there?" I slightly pointed in Anthony's direction.

"Yeah. What about him?" from the look on William's face, he wasn't impressed.

"That's my psycho ex., I was just about to tell you about him."

Next thing I knew, I looked to my left and Anthony was standing right next to me. Damn it!

"Well looky here, "Anthony says with a devilish grin, "How are you, Courtni?"

"I'm fine. Thank you for asking. Well, it's great seeing you. Have a good evening. Goodbye!" I replied. I wish he would walk away already. He stood there looking at William with jealousy in his eyes.

"Who this?" he said. He almost looked surprised to see me on a date.

"I'm William Masterton," he stands up and approaches an eye level with Anthony, "And this is a private table. Have a nice evening, sir."

"A man with class, or is it an act?"

"A man with much more class than you." William replied. William stood up from the table and got in Anthony's face. Something tells me that this is going to be a perfect dinner ruined.

"Don't toy with me boy! You need to raise up out my face before you get smacked down on your ass!" said Anthony.

"Oh, you think so?"

"I know so, pretty boy!"

"I like a man with courage, but not only are you about to get your feelings hurt, you're also about to be thrown out of my restaurant."

"So, it is true that old man Masterton had a son. I should have known since you look like a pretty, rich boy version of that country bumpkin!"

"Yeah but this pretty rich boy is fine dining with one of the most beautiful ladies in this establishment, while you walked up in here with a broke ass two dollar whore."

The whole restaurant went, "Damn!" There was even a gentleman in the back that said, "Yeah that is an ugly bitch he walked in here with." I was trying my best to keep it together and not laugh. I'm not big on men arguing or fighting over women, but this was some funny shit.

"I refuse to be seen here with a punk," said Anthony's date while walking over to our table. Now that I had gotten a closer look, she wasn't hitting on anything! She really did look like a two dollar whore. "A punk who allows a restaurant owner and his patrons to disrespect me. I'm leaving!"

"Baby wait!" Anthony tried to go after her, but she was already out the door. He stormed back to the table like a little kid. "You embarrassed me in front of my gal, man!"

"No, I believe you embarrassed yourself." William replied.

"Courtni, you need to get your little rich pet under control."

"I don't need to do anything," I replied, "You started it! I really think you should get your meal somewhere else. I could always call the police, since they are looking for you."

"Oh, it's like that, huh? You ain't supposed to be out with another man no way!"

"Says who? You? You're done telling me what to do, or who I can go any place with! Last time I checked, I am grown, therefore, I can go wherever the hell I want!"

"Damn right says me! You're supposed to be in the house crying your eyes out over our break-up."

"WRONG! I am right where I'm supposed to be! And besides, also the last I checked, I broke up with you. So, why should I be the one at home crying?"

"Who the fuck you talking to like that, bitch?"

Just as Anthony was about to raise his hand to slap me, William grabbed his hand.

"I know you are not about to hit a woman, especially this one! I've had just about enough! Don't you ever talk to her or any woman like that in my presence! Furthermore, you better not raise your hand to a female. You know...hold on...Malik! Gustavo! Get this bastard out of my restaurant! Got me cursing in front of my patrons and my lady --"

These two, extremely large, muscle bound men, stood on both sides of Anthony. They picked him up and carried him to the front door. Anthony shouted, "You haven't seen the last of me. Especially you, bitch!" The entire restaurant started clapping and shouting. I was so relieved after Anthony was tossed out on his butt. Any other day I would be embarrassed, but considering I had this awesome man standing up for me and the entire restaurant cheering for him, it made it all okay.

"You really didn't have to stick up for me, but thank you."

"Yes, I did have to stand up for you. That is something I do not tolerate under any circumstances. A man who disrespects a woman that is a respectable woman is a fool." William said, "What happened between you two anyway?"

"It's very similar to your story, but just add violence. In a sick way, I thought he loved me. I had it bad for him, and he played me. Anthony took advantage of the feelings I did have. I was truly blinded by the small, yet good things he did in our relationship. In the end, they weren't good enough, and I called it off. I know it was the best, for me, and that I do deserve better. Sometimes though, William, it hurts like hell knowing that I was that stupid and even the fact that I miss him sometimes. "

"The violence part is bad enough. No one deserves to be treated like he treated you tonight."

"Please, tonight was a good night in comparison to some of the other stuff in the past."

"No matter what happens with us Courtni, do not let any other man take your confidence and your self-worth away from you. When that happens, you are more open to abuse, and you do not deserve that. Promise me, okay?"

"Okay, I promise."

"Don't trip off of him, though. I'll treat you right, if you let me."

"I don't know. There are things --"

"We will take it slow. This is a road of discovery for both of us. We both have been through things that we regret, and if we could, we would do over. Neither one of us need to jump into any committed relationships until we work through the problem areas that allowed us to be in those bad relationships to begin with. I cannot deny that I like you, and I have this feeling that the Lord sent me you. If I'm wrong, I still want to prove to you that I can be a better man than that Anthony character. If we are meant to be together, we will be. If not, then you'll at least know that there are still some good men in the world, and you don't have to settle."

"We'll see. Time will tell."

After that, William drove me home. The ride was very quiet. I was lost in my thoughts, and I'm sure he had plenty on his mind as well. As I replayed the events of what happened during the evening, I just couldn't believe that I was ever that stupid to be with a man like Anthony. Well, everybody plays the fool once or twice in their lives. Before I knew it, we were in front of my house. William got out, opened the car door for me, and walked me up to the front door.

"I had a great time tonight," said William, "In spite of Anthony."

"Yeah, me too. He didn't scare you away from me, did he?"

"Not a chance! Like I said before, I'm sticking around if you let me. In fact, when can I see you again?"

"After tonight, William I don't know --"

"Please, call me Wil. You don't have to be so formal."

"There are things about my relationship with Anthony, I wasn't able to tell you about due to our interruption. There are things about Anthony in general I really need to tell you about. He has a history of being crazy and very dangerous. I didn't find out these things until three months into the relationship. If anything were to happen to you because of him, I wouldn't be able to live with myself."

"The last thing I'm worried about is Anthony."

"Well, you really should be. You have no idea what he is capable of."

"There's not a man in this world that can scare me. The only person I fear is God, the Father of all Creations. Besides, it's not anyone's fault that he's jealous. Please, let me do this. Let me show you the kind of man I can be. The kind of man that you need and deserve in your life."

"Look, it's late. I will call you tomorrow."

"Okay then. Goodnight, Courtni."

He kissed my cheek, and then left. I stood at the door, watching him get in his car and drive away. I was thinking to myself, what a wonderful man. Do I deserve him? Before we went out, I was excited but still hesitant. I didn't want to be blinded again like I was with Anthony. The one thing that gives me comfort is that I have peace in my soul, and the impression that he is genuine. All the times I was with Anthony, there was something inside holding me back. Whispers were telling me to not be with him, not go places, and not to sleep with him. I was stubborn and did what I wanted to do, which has brought me to this point: fearful of relationships and even fearful knowing that Anthony knows I am attempting to date. If I let myself fall for Wil, or any man for that matter, he will try to do something to destroy it. With all my heart, I don't want that, especially with Wil. A part of me wants to call him and say, "Sorry I can't do this." But those same voices that were in my head telling me not to be with Anthony are whispering, "Be still and know."

Chapter Four

I woke up the next morning to beautiful sunshine and the ocean breeze waiting for me to embrace it. Saturdays are normally the days I enjoy the most. Today, I was conflicted on account of my date last night. I enjoyed my time with William, but Anthony came along and ruined it. No matter what I try to do, he seems to always linger when I'm trying to let go. Why won't he go away? How can I live my life without him? I have no desire to take him back, but I don't have the deal with the drama that comes with him. I felt a tear run down my cheek. I knew this weren't tears of sadness, but more of tears on anger.

I had to get my mind off of my aggression towards Anthony. I picked up the phone to call Malova. I'm sure she would be dying to hear about what went down last night. What makes her so awesome is that she would care more about what happened between me and William versus the drama with Anthony.

"Hey lady, I got some news for you."

"I know some of it already. You went out with Wil and Anthony brought a date and busted up the party." I held the phone, feeling perplexed. Then again, I shouldn't be surprised. Anthony always did gossip like a girl.

"How did you-"

"Your crazy ex called me last night and told me about how William had him thrown out."

"That's true. There was a reason for that."

"He said you and William were frontin' on him. You embarrassed him in front of Tasha."

"So, that's the two-dollar hoes' name?"

"Why does she have to be all that?"Malova started laughing.

"That's what Wil called her last night. Actually, he called her a whore, but it all means the same thing. He was more proper with it."

"If William called her a whore, then she must have been bad. I've heard about Tasha but I've never seen her."

"Yeah, well you aren't missing much, honey. Now, back to the frontin' part of your comment; there was a reason for that too!"

"I know, girl. Anthony always twists the truth to make himself look good. That's why he and my estranged brother get along so damn well. What really happened?"

"Alright, Wil and I were having dinner at La Bonita - which he owns by the way."

"That surprises me a bit. He didn't come off as the well-to-do type when I approached him at the beach."

"Yeah, but he's very modest about it, and it appears that he likes to keep it on the hush. Anyway, we were having a great conversation about his family and our past. Right when I was about to tell him about Anthony, the bastard walks in with his date."

"Talk about bad timing."

"Bad timing is an understatement. I wanted to leave right then and there, but I didn't want to make it obvious that I was attempting to run away. Well, Anthony comes up in the restaurant like he owns the place. Then, he comes over to our table and starts to harass us. Wil told him off, and Anthony's date got embarrassed and left. Anthony was still trying to talk shit. Wil broke him off some more, but he still was talking shit. Before I knew it, Malik and Gustavo were carrying Anthony out the door."

"Who are Malik and Gustavo?"

"They were at the beach the same day you embarrassed me and got Wil's number. I also think that they work at the restaurant as bouncers. Back to the story, which is coming to a close, they threw Anthony out on his ass. Serves him right!"

"That was some quality entertainment you experienced. Oh well, he'll be alright. Now, back to you missy, you're calling him Wil now?"

"Yeah, I guess so."

"Do you like him?"

"Of course I do -- especially after what he did for me last night. So far, he's really been a breath of fresh air."

"Alright already. Save the soft stuff for someone that wants to hear all that. Have you told him that?"

"Not exactly. He has a good impression that I like him."

"Impressions aren't good enough. You need to be clear with that man."

"That might be true, but right now all I need is a friend. At this point, I'm scared to even have that with Anthony lurking about."

"You can't stop living life because someone else is trying to dictate it for you. If you want something, you got to go out and get it. In this case, you don't even have to go anywhere, he's in your face, and he's already fighting for you."

"I know. I just need some time to."

"He isn't going to wait around forever, you know."

"If he likes me as much as he says he does, he will."

I heard a knock at my front door. Who could be coming over unannounced? Wil doesn't strike me as that kind of person and the only person I know that would do that is on the phone with me.

"I'll call you back, Malova."

"Alright then; think about what I just told you."

"Yeah right! Bye."

I cracked the door slightly and Anthony barged his way in. He started roaming around the house instantly -- almost like he was looking for something, or someone.

"You didn't have to front me off like you did last night," he says, "you made me look like a damn fool."

"You made yourself look like a fool," I said, "You came to a private table being disruptive. A hi and bye was all you had to do. Or better yet, how about you should have gone about your business with your date! Maybe you could have gotten laid last night or something instead of wasting your Saturday morning tormenting me."

"Yeah you're right -- I could have gotten laid last night if you and your...whatever he is hadn't scared my date off."

"You got everything you deserve last night, so you can leave my house now and take your pity party with you!"

"How was I supposed to act seeing you with another man?"

"How did you think I felt when I saw you with those other women? Even so, it doesn't matter now because we are not together. I have the right to see whoever I want and so do you. Besides, why do you care? According to my sources, you were going to dump me anyway. I believe the term I was informed of was you were going to write me off; like I'm some type of tax deduction. Do you remember saying that?"

"It was nothing personal."

"Nothing personal? It was personal to me. I loved you. I was committed to you. I would have given you everything I could. I gave you everything and you played me out like an eight track. You had no respect for me or my body. When I found out from Varsha and Greg, I was hurt. Thank God I didn't get pregnant or worse, get AIDS! Do you not think STD's exist? I know one thing, if I would have caught something it would have been your --"

"Bitch please! You wouldn't have done--"

"I am tired of you shutting me down! This is my house and my life! I will no longer tolerate you disrespecting me! I've decided to move on without you. I thought you would have been happy that I was slowing you down or nagging you. Now that I'm moving on without you, you're mad and feel disrespected? It's time for a reality check – I do not care about your feelings! Did you really think I was going to live out the rest of my life begging you to love me? Be with me? I'm tired of fighting for us. I chose to dump you before you could dump me, and I am a better person for it, too! Even if you weren't going to dump me, I still would have done it because you violated our relationship the moment you decided to give yourself to another woman!"

"I'm a man, Courtni! That's what we do!"

"You had no reason to! You could have had me any time you wanted to. You were the one telling me no!"

"I needed something new. I was tired of your stuff."

"That's cold, Anthony. But then again, what could I expect from a world class thug? It's cool though. Like I said, I'm tired of fighting for us. I'm in a decent place with someone that seems to appreciate the woman that's in front of him, - something you never could do."

"Whatever! You'll regret this decision. You'll want me back, and when you do I'll decide if I want to put up with your games!"

"Anthony, I will never regret my decision!"

"Oh you will, once you discover that none of these other cats will put up with you. Who sent you those pictures anyway?"

"It doesn't matter who sent them to me. What matters is that you get out of my life and my house!"

"Do you think I'm stupid? I know Varsha has that detective agency! Your friends should have minded their own business."

"Regardless of how I received it, I'm glad the information was forwarded to me. If not, I would have probably continued to play your fool while you lied to me day in and day out!"

"If you wanted honesty, I could have given it to you. Yeah, I played you. A part of me did care about you, but you were too easy, so I treated you like one of my hoes. You want to know how I treat hoes? I make them fall in love with me, fuck them, get them pregnant, and leave their lonely asses. The first two went according to plan. Thanks to some nosey ass person, the rest of it was shot to hell."

"You're unbelievable! You're nothing but a dog, but you can go and find another dog house. I hate you. I never want to see you again. Get out of my house and out of my life. Get out!"

I heard footsteps behind me. I turned around and it was Wil. I was so in rapture with my anger that I totally forgot I left the door wide open. He had a dozen red roses in his hand with a look of fury on his face. I could tell by his facial expression that he most likely heard everything, or at least enough to invoke aggravation.

"Normally I would call first," said Wil as he threw my flowers on the couch and started pacing my living room, "but I was in the neighborhood, and I was just going to drop these off. Now that I see your harassment tactics are a way of life for you, Tony, I'm glad I stopped by."

"Only my friends call me Tony and you, pretty boy, are not one of them."

"You are a sorry excuse for a man. You used her like a toy. You ought to be ashamed of yourself."

"This is none of your business, man! Damn, it seems every time I try to have a conversation with my lady, you wanna' show up and shit." Anthony pushed my favorite Tiffany vase off the coffee table. Damn him!

"She's no longer your lady. That was clearly established last night, as far as I am concerned. Now, I know I don't own anything in this house, but I think I clearly speak for Courtni when I say get out of this house. Oh, as well as her confirming she wanted you out with her screaming *get out*." He walked up to Anthony slowly until he was gazing at him with a cold stare. "Don't come back. Don't call or speak to her ever again."

"What are you, her guardian now or something?"

"It's none of your business what I am to her. All you need to concern yourself with is leaving."

"Listen here, my brother. I don't have anything against you. In fact, you seem like you can be cool people. With your money and status in the community, you can have any woman you want. Why waste your time with this one?"

"You don't know anything about me."

"I know more about you than you realize. I make it my business to be resourceful."

"Well you and your resourcefulness need to check yourself before you start building profiles on people. You may think you know me, but you have no idea what I'm about."

"I know enough to know that you're too good for Courtni."

"Worry about yourself. I know how to take care of things, and I especially know how to take care of a lady." Wil walked over to me and out his arms around me. I wanted to melt in his arms right in front of Anthony, "I'm where I want to be."

"You bitch-ass --"

"You know, you really need to chill with the name calling. Sticks and stones -- didn't your mother ever teach you that? Furthermore, you can do all the name calling and issuing of empty threats that you want to do. When it's all said and done, I'm a better man than you any day of the year. In fact, I know drug dealers that have more integrity than you."

"Brother, how about you get out and let me and Courtni work through our issues!"

"How about…no! And, I'm not your damn brother, homey -- none of that! This is your final warning to get out of here. I am getting really tired of being civil – especially since you're not taking the hint! Focus on your life and leave us alone. Besides, from what I heard, you didn't want to be with her anyway, so why are you worried about who she's with?"

"I'm going to say this one last time -- stay away from Courtni, and no one gets hurt."

"That's it! It seems like your type will only respond to violence. You're going to leave – either willingly or you'll be removed by force."

"Oh, I'd like to see that, rich boy!"

Wil grabbed Anthony by the throat and lifted him above his head. On the left side of his forehead, I noticed a blue vein bulging out. The fear of death was on Anthony's face as he started to turn pale. The vixen in me was enjoying the show, but I know this was wrong. I walked up to Wil, placing my hand on his shoulder. I looked up at him with concerned eyes. He looked down at me, and he could tell that I wanted him to turn Anthony loose.

"Are you enjoying this as much as I am?"

"I'll leave," Anthony said faintly, "I'll leave!" Wil threw Anthony to the floor. He scurried on his feet and started walking towards his motorcycle. "Okay, I see you want to play around. Mark my words, we all are going to play, and I'm going to be the one having fun. You're a dead, rich boy. Just wait and see."

Anthony jumped on his bike and rode off into the blazing sunlight. I couldn't believe what just happened. I was so heated. I wanted so badly to chase after him and run him over on my bike. Even though I have no interest in being with Anthony ever again, it still hurt to listen to him admit that he played me. I was nothing but a hoe to him. Then he had the nerve to define the word hoe. Then he says, "I care." If what he did to me was caring, then love must be deadly. I'm so glad I left that relationship. Wil was standing by the door. He still looked really pissed off. Anthony has a tendency to bring that out in people. I walked over to him and hugged him.

"Hey, are you all right?"

"Yeah, I'm cool. Better question is, are you okay?"

"Yeah, just a painful reminder that I did the right thing when I walked away from him."

"I really don't like that dude."

"Join the club. Once again, thanks for being my knight in shining armor. It really means a lot to me."

"Was he always like that during your relationship with him?"

"In the beginning, no. He was a cheap-skate, but he was sweet. About three months into the relationship, that's when he got all crazy and stuff, being verbally and physically abusive. Guess that's what I get for dating a smooth criminal."

"There you go, downing yourself again."

"Sorry. It's a bad habit of mine. The thing is, I know I should have gotten out when he started acting that way. However, I didn't; therefore, in a sense I got what I deserved."

"Like I told you about my deal with Francis, walk away from the Anthony situation learning something about the relationship and don't make the same mistake."

"Trust me, I have. I've learned far too much and quite frankly the lesson could have been avoided."

"The things we endure in life are placed before us to make us stronger."

"Wil, let me ask you something."

"Sure things, but first…" He handed me the roses he brought over. They were beautiful. I haven't received flowers since high school. Anthony was too cheap to buy flowers. His theory was there's no point to pay over twenty-five dollars for something that will die in seven days or less.

"Thank you. The flowers are lovely."

"You're welcome. Do you mind if I sit down?"

"Of course not." He sat down on the couch. After putting the flowers in some water, I sat down next to him. "Look, I've got to ask you – why do you still want to deal me?"

"Why wouldn't I?"

"Do you really want me to state the obvious here?"

"That thing that left here was not a reflection of you. It's a reflection of a past that needs to stay there."

"Agreed, but to even continue being friends you'll have to deal with him, to a point. He's not going to go away just because you choked him. That's going to give him more ammunition to make my life a living hell."

"Then he'll just have to get choked over and over until he gets the message."

"I'm being serious here."

"I know you are –"

"Why deal with the drama? Why not get to know someone that can give you a drama free relationship?"

"There's no such thing as drama free relationships. The slightest disagreement you have with someone is considered drama -- no matter how big or small."

"My situation goes well beyond big drama."

"Why don't you let me decide? It seems like you're trying to make up my mind for me."

"That's not it. I just don't want to walk away in the middle of us getting started with something. If you're going to leave, I'd rather you do it now while I'll understand why. Most men wouldn't want to deal with this."

"I'm not most men. Look, I know it may seem that I don't know you very well, but I genuinely care about you." He took me into his arms and gazed into my eyes. His deep, dark eyes seemed to pierce my soul -- not the wrathful eyes that were staring at Anthony in mid-air. "I know you've been hurt, I heard the entire argument. Just remember, what goes around comes around and when it comes back on him, I'd love to be a fly on the wall."

"As long as you're willing to share some wall space with me, it's all good." We both started laughing. He grabbed my hand. I felt his energy coursing through my body. It took my breath away. I couldn't believe that I could have all of these different feelings for a person I barely knew. I never felt this way before, and it scares me a little.

"I'm not looking for you to give me a lifetime commitment, but maybe someday I'll ask for that. Right now, all I want to do is stick around and be your friend. Don't be like most women and push me away because of your bad experience. "

"I don't want to push you away, but I'm afraid. There's a part of me that is begging – screaming even for you to be in my life as more than a friend. The other part of me is telling me to run and not look back. I don't want to rush into anything, but I don't want you ending our friendship because of my ex and his bull."

"If I were to ever leave, it would be because you pushed me so far away that I couldn't reach you anymore."

"I'm not trying to push…"

"Stop pushing." He touched my face. He looked as if he wanted to kiss me. I wanted to kiss him, but I couldn't move. "You're going to have to be patient with me."

"I'm willing, but even I have my limitations."

"I understand, but know this -- I want you in my life. You're doing a great job as a friend, when the time is right, I won't object to us being more than that. The thing is, I don't know when that time will come."

"If it's meant to be, then we'll both know that it's right. Running away won't even be a thought."

He placed both of his hands on my face. They were so warm and inviting. At that moment, I went to kiss him, but he pulled away to get something in his pocket. I regained my composure, so it wouldn't look obvious that I was about to put the moves on him. It's probably best anyway. I'm so confused. He stood up and took a step backwards. He pulled out a business card and handed it to me. I looked at it with confusion.

"The other real reason why I came over with flowers, before all the excitement, was to tell you that I have to go to Mississippi for awhile." he said with a sad look.

"What's going on? Is everything okay?"

"My dad is in the hospital. Mom says he's pretty bad." Whew! Not whew about his dad, but I'm glad it has nothing to do with Anthony.

"Oh, I am so sorry to hear that. I will make sure to say a prayer for you and your family tonight."

"Thank you. I never turn down prayer invitations. You've won another favor in my eyesight."

"Why is that?" I started giggling and blushing.

"I figured you were a believer, but it's not always good to assume. You just proved it though."

"Yeah, I am a believer. I don't always act like it but He is in my heart always."

"Amen to that!"

"Is there anything I can do for you during this time period besides pray?"

"Actually there is. Don't forget about me because there won't be a day that goes by when I'm not thinking of you. Don't lose this card because it has my parent's address and phone number. I plan on talking to you every day and even writing you sometimes."

"Writing? Wil, how long are you going to be gone?"

"About a month. If this is really dad's home-going, then there's a lot of stuff that I'm going to have to do with his property down there and even all the businesses he owns."

"Oh, okay I see there's an email address on here. Can I email you?"

"Of course you can. I wasn't talking about using snail mail."

"Yeah, you got to love technology." The back of my throat felt constricted. My breathing hastened. My eyes felt like bees were stinging them. I can't believe that I'm getting this emotionally attached to this man. This is the reason why I want to push him away. This can't be good to have these feelings this fast. He hasn't even left and I already miss him.

"One more thing, if Merrick shows his face around you, call me. I'll make sure Malik and Gustavo take care of him. Promise me you'll call?"

"I Promise."

"I meant everything I said Courtni. I'll call you when I get to Mississippi. Enjoy your flowers."

Wil kissed me on my forehead and left. I sat on my couch lifeless. Well, I appeared lifeless on the outside. Internally, I was suffering, nervous and dizzy. It felt like a fairy was waving a wand – casting spells all around my heart. This enchantment was causing me to be afraid of myself and my thoughts of Wil. Our conversation today kept playing over and over in my head. Maybe this time apart is what I need. I need to sort through my demons before this goes any further.

Chapter Five

Wil had been gone for three weeks, and it feels like it's been three years. I missed him so much, but I didn't dare to tell him. It doesn't matter – in my heart I feel that he knows... Even though we talked on IM, email and had frequent phone calls, it still doesn't replace him being here. During the times we couldn't talk, I threw myself into my work. My reputation was starting to build in the community, and I was getting a lot of requests from celebrities -- especially after my shoot with Nora Kennedy. I was even thinking of saving money and purchasing my own studio versus being on call with several companies.

Around 8 P.M. my cell phone went off. I didn't have to look at it to know it was Wil. I had his ring tone set to "Nothing Compares to You" by Sinead O'Connor.

"Hey Mr. Masterton. How are things going?" I asked.

"A little bit crazy, but in the end I'm blessed. Dad's surgery was a success, but they were concerned with him not snapping out of the anesthesia right away. My mom is a wreck because she's trying to keep Dad off his feet. He's so used to taking care of her that he can't adjust to being taken care of."

"Every time you talk about your parents, they remind me of how mine was. They would probably still be that way if my mother was alive."

"I can tell you miss her a lot. Just remember the good times and the wonderful life that she lived. After she served her purpose, God called her home."

"Yeah, I know. But, let's not talk about that. Finish telling me about your craziness that's occurring."

"I had to handle twelve evictions in the apartment complex that we own down here, and to top things off, I am missing you."

"You say that every time we talk."

"Well, it's the truth. I can't wait to get back home to see you."

"I'd rather you show me rather than tell me."

"Is that an offer, Ms. Taylor?"

"Maybe. When you get home, try and find out."

"It's a deal. How was your day? Meet any more famous people?"

"Yeah, I was requested to do a shoot for Ucal Quail. He wasn't a joy to work with because he had to have everything his way. He had the nerve to try and tell me that he didn't like my camera, and that I need a new one ASAP!"

"Are you serious?"

"I am. It took everything I had to not set him straight and walk off the set. I kept my composure, and it turned out to be the best. He gave my card to Naam Davenport."

"Isn't that dude that played in Four Times a Man?"

"The same one. He claims that he will call me in three weeks to set up a time to meet and go over his terms for the shoot."

"That's good, baby!"

"When did I become your baby?" I started smiling, but I didn't want him to know it.

"Sorry if I offended you -- the words came out naturally."

"I was just asking. There's no need to apologize."

"Well, what if I told you that I wanted you to be my baby?"

"Then I would tell you that you need to save that conversation for in person. To me, it would have more value if I could look you in your eyes while you tell me that."

"That's a fair assessment and request."

"Have you been thinking about asking me?" I couldn't resist but to ask the question. I hope I don't pay for it later.

"I would have to say yes. You are a really cool, inspiring and an attractive woman. The only thing that holds me back from seriously approaching you is because there are still a bunch of questions that I need to answer within myself. I do not want to rush into a relationship with anyone. In your case, you are everything I could ever want, but I want to make sure this is right. I've been praying and meditating to be shown who my wife will be."

"Wow, that's deep. I don't know what to say to that."

"There's nothing much to say about it. All I know is that I am waiting for the Lord to speak to me with regards to my relationship with you. Once he does, I will act according to his will."

"That's the best course of action to take. I will pray for revelations regarding what you're seeking. I honestly need to be doing the same thing for myself. I am at a good place in my life. He has blessed me with so much! Right now the missing piece in my life is that special someone to share it with. I will be honest and tell you that I pray that it's you."

"I am flattered. I'll lift you up in prayer as well."

"Thank you."

"I don't mean to venture from our lovely subject, but have you heard from Anthony?"

"No I haven't. I am thankful."

"That eases my mind a lot. I have to be honest with you about something."

"What's that?"

"I've been having Malik and Gustavo check up on you as well as Anthony. Seems like he's been dodging the law. I heard through my assistant manager at La Bonita that the evidence has come back on the night club bombing. He's been able to dodge every lead that the cops have on him. So good, in fact, that he's featured on Long Beach Most Wanted last night."

"I'm not surprised at all. I'm just happy that part of my life is behind me. I am looking forward to a new day."

"Amen to that. Well, I got to get off of here. I have some papers and other documentation to sign. I will call you tomorrow."

"Okay, well you have a good night."

"I will."

We said our goodnights, and I hung up the phone. I sat down on my couch and stretched my arms. I had an overwhelming feeling of peace and goodness when I think of my life with him. On the other hand, I feel disturbed. The thought of Wil fills my heart with excitement and joy. At the same time, my mind was creating a sense of nervousness within me. What if we never became more than friends? Would I be okay with that? When the time is right, I want it to be more. But would God approve?

I got off the couch and went to my bedroom. I got down on my knees and prayed to the Lord to bless Wil's family, Wil's desire for a wife and my desires for Wil. Right as I said "Amen", the phone started ringing. I just knew it was Wil calling me back. He normally does to tell me a joke of some sort, so he can hear me laugh.

"So what's the joke of the evening?" I asked grinning from ear to ear.

"You have a correctional facility call from -- Courtni it's Tone, pick up!" What the he--? I can't believe it's this fool! I went from being in a joy luck mood to being angry in all of five seconds. I wanted to hang up the phone and ignore the call, but I knew if I did, then he would keep calling until I spoke to him. The automated system asked, Will you accept the charges? I reluctantly said yes.

"Yo baby! I'm down in Avenal! Come let me out!"

"I know you're not calling me. Call one of your groupies to get you out of jail."

"Because you are the only one with money and still the only one who's allowed to get into my house to get the money for me. Come on now, Courtni; bail a brother out of jail."

"I am not bailing you out of anything. What you got is a personal problem that doesn't concern me.""

"Look, I know we've been through some things and the way we left things two weeks ago wasn't all that hot. All I can do now is tell you I'm sorry, and that I will be a changed man when I get out of here."

"Are you hard of hearing? I said it's not my problem!"

"Damn Courtni. What I got to do? Beg?"

"No because there's isn't enough groveling in the world that you could do that would even make me think of bailing you out of jail. I am curious to know how you got locked up."

"I was making a run with Daidus when the police pulled us over because he was doing 105 in a 75 mile per hour zone. The officer recognized my face from that whack ass Long Beach Most Wanted clip and he cuffed me."

"So you were responsible for the bombing of The Whiz?"

"I am not at liberty to discuss that without my lawyer being present."

"You are amazing to me." If my face could turn red, it would have been as red as a beet. He has the nerve to call me after everything he has put me through, and now I know that I was in love or lust with a murderer? Lord, forgive me for my stupidity! This is exactly why I shouldn't have taken the call. I'm upset for nothing. This could have been avoided. My mouth says that I've let go, but this proves that I haven't. Why can't I end this crazy connection? It's proven over and over that it's unhealthy, but yet I keep putting myself through this. I need to be stronger. I need to completely let go. "I am a fool for taking this phone call. Call someone else because I am not going to bail you out of jail. Goodnight!"

I slammed the phone onto the receiver. I can't believe I wasted ten minutes on that conversation. I really thought I was healing and moving on from this situation with Anthony. I'm not. The worse thing in all this is there's a wonderful, caring, compassionate man that's willing to be with me. I want to be with him, but not while I still have these conflicting emotions. I miss Wil, but I'm glad he's not around to see me going through these emotions. Though I'm not jumping in my car to go and bail Anthony out, I'm still allowing him to rule my life. I feel like a caged bird, that's being held prisoner. I want my independence. I want to be free, but how can I do that? The phone started ringing again. I checked the caller ID, and it was Wil. Whew!

"Hey there." I said – still relieved that it wasn't Anthony calling back.

"Hi – you okay? You sound a little bothered."

"No, I'm fine. Just trying to get ready for bed is all."

"Oh, well I won't keep you. I wanted to tell you that I have to stay two more weeks down here,"

"Is everything all right?" This was the last thing I needed to hear. I was looking forward to him coming back home soon.

"Everything is cool. I just have some additional things I need to take care of while I'm down here. I won't be coming back as soon as I would have liked to."

"I understand about taking care of things."

"Are you okay? I'm starting to think you're really not. Did I jinx you by mentioning Anthony?"

"Somewhat, but no matter. He's in jail."

"Good ridden then."

"Anyways, take care of your business. It's not like I won't talk to for two weeks."

"This is true. I did want to let you know at least what was up."

"I appreciate that."

"Well, I'm off to bed. If you need anything from me, call me at any time."

"I will. Have a good night."

In the passing weeks, I heard nothing from Anthony. I was thankful for that. I talked to Wil on IM or through email, which is always welcomed. He said he had a lot of things to finish so he didn't have time to talk on the phone. At this rate I didn't care because hearing from him period was good enough for me. I missed him so much. I knew in a matter of days I could gaze into his eyes and enter a trance of serenity. I honestly can say I've never felt this way about anyone. My heart sings and dances just at the mere thought of him.

I now question if I truly loved Anthony. I put up with a lot of things that I shouldn't have, and I claimed it all for love. Now, I wonder why I did put up with it. The way I feel about Wil; I didn't feel these things for Anthony. As I truly sit back and think about my relationship with Anthony, all it encompassed was fun parties, good sex, and I could technically say that I had someone in my life. All that came with a price of being betrayed, belittled and life threatening. So why did I stay as long as I did? How could I have loved a monster? There was no intimacy, ever, in our relationship. Though we were together, often, in the beginning I felt alone most of the time. Towards the end, I felt alone and abused. He would threaten my life constantly, and I was so afraid that he would kill me. That's it! I was afraid. Not just of what he would do but of many things. I was afraid of being alone. Afraid to start over again with someone new; in fear that they would be worse than Anthony. The feeling I thought was love for Anthony, was nothing but lust and self imprisonment. I hate that it took me this long to realize it, but now I know what not to do again.

The experience of enlightenment is always beneficial. Regardless of how things end with Wil, I am thankful he's in my life. I feel like I'm in a relationship, even though we haven't made that step. I can breathe, show my face; I can smile. The thought of Wil gives me a sense of openness and freedom. For the first time in a long time, I have free will. I deserve a satisfying, healthy life.

There's still fear of being hurt, but I'm not going to allow fear to hold me hostage. I'm not sure what the future holds, but I think its time I move forward – with Wil. Life is about living and learning. Considering all the things I went through with Anthony, it was a lesson well learned. New lessons and memories will be made with Wil in my life.

I couldn't wait to tell my friends about my decision to pursue Wil. I knew that not only would they be happy, they would also support me. If it hadn't been for my friends, I wouldn't have left Anthony alone nor met Wil in the first place. I knew Varsha would be at home for sure, so I decided to call her first.

"Hello, is Varsha there?"

"This is her, Courtni," she replied, "I'm the only female living here."

"It's habit. I deal with clients on the phone all day."

"Yeah, well if I ever became one of your clients, please talk to me like you normally talk to me."

I started chuckling at her dry humor, "You can cut the sarcasm. I have some news for you and the rest of the gang."

"You sound really excited about this. Is this why you've been hiding out for a month? Did Anthony get hit by a tow truck or something?"

"Girl I can tell you something even better! He called me from jail two weeks ago!"

"Are you serious?"

"Heck yeah I'm serious. He had the nerve to ask me to bail him out of jail. Can you believe the nerve?"

"With Anthony, yes I can believe it. You've been helping him out of trouble all this time. Why would things change?"

"Because I've changed. Girl, I was sitting here thinking about everything that went on in my relationship, and then I started thinking about my friendship with Wil. Even though a commitment isn't in place between Wil and I, there's sanctuary from all the crazy crap, I allowed Anthony to put me through. I'm done with him, and anyone that would act like him. I'm not doing that to myself again."

"Honey, I'm glad to hear that. What did you tell him when he asked you to bail him out?"

"No, and him being in jail was not my problem. He wasn't happy with that, but his displeasure no longer affects me."

"This conversation is making me extremely happy."

"Well how about you come over tomorrow afternoon to engage in more extremely happy conversation while eating my signature Florentine ring?"

"You know I can never say no to the Florentine ring. I'll grab everyone and haul them over."

"Cool! Will see ya tomorrow then."

The next day I prepared lunch and margaritas. They all came over about 2:15 P.M., and they were all hungry. While they were stuffing their faces, I took the time to catch up on the missed events of my friends' lives. Malova came over and placed her hand on my forehead like, she was checking my temperature.

"Alright girly, what's the biggy?" asked Malova. "Not trying to say it isn't good to see you and all, but we haven't heard a hide tail of you in a while and Varsha says you've lost your mind."

"Not exactly. I've had a lot of work these past couple of weeks."

"That's understandable, but I feel there's more than what you are telling so spill it." declared Mike.

"I'm with Mike on that one. You're all smiling and shit. What's gotten into you, girl?" asked Greg.

"Okay folks, here's the deal." I started, "Remember a month ago, Malova when we were on the phone, and I told you I'd call you back?"

"Yeah, and you never did!" replied Malova.

"Well, it was Anthony at the door. He barged in my house, started yelling and breakin' stuff because he was jealous that I was out with Wil."

"Wil, huh? You guys are on a nickname basis, I see." said Varsha.

"Yeah, we are, and it's very nice, too."

"Oh!" everyone shouted.

"Shut up and listen! Then, he was all like, *I can't see other men and breaking up with me wasn't anything personal.* I went off, and the truth came out. I could have really gone on with life without seeing his true colors. That relationship was a waste of time. He was using me and he admitted to it."

"Why that no good son of a bit--"Varsha placed her hand over Greg's mouth. He gave her a cold glare, but then softened his eyes and calmed down.

"No good doesn't even begin to describe him. In the midst of the yelling, I must have forgotten to close my door and next thing, I know, Wil is standing there with flowers in his hand and a look of frustration. He heard everything! I thought he went off on Anthony at the restaurant, but not like he did at my house. Wil ate Anthony's pride for breakfast. Furthermore, he damn near choked the boy in my living room!"

"Man I wish I could have been there for that one. Something told me I should have come over that night." said Malova.

"The important thing is that you are okay, and he got the message." said Mike.

"So, let's talk about Wil," Malova said grinning like a kid with candy, "Sounds like things are getting serious with you two. And yet, it took you a month to tell us? What's been going on all this time?"

"Well, he's been gone because his dad is sick, so he's taking care of business there. We still talk everyday, which is nice. He's even sent me cards and other tangible displays of affection. He's just so wonderful, more than I ever expected. The bound that we have is no other I've ever experienced. If this is what true love feels like, then I've never had it. I want to keep it, but I'm scared. I've played different scenarios over in my head, both good and bad. I want to take the chance, but I don't want to regret it. If I walk away, then I could lose something that I may never have again."

"Babe, you'll never know unless you try. From what you've told us, I don't see a reason why you wouldn't try." Malova approached me and grabbed my hand. "Life is about risks and chances. Some will be good. Others, not so much, but you live on, and you learn. When I decided to get with Mike, I felt everything you felt. Yeah, we all know that I got on him for running, but now I'm thankful he did. Both of us needed to take care of personal issues. Now, we take care of each other. Everything you're feeling right now I understand. Varsha does also. Look at how things turned out for us?"

"True but you all had the advantage of having a tenure friendship."

"That doesn't mean a damn thing. I've known people that thought they knew someone because they'd been around them for ten years and on, but when the relationship started, they didn't know each other at all. I've also seen the opposite. The bottom line, what does your heart tell you?"

"I want to be with him. I want to find out where this is going. I care about him, and I know that the feeling isn't one sided. Despite my fears, I don't want to be without him."

"It's about time," Varsha was saying, "The lonely girl has opened her heart again."

"I'm proud of you." said Greg.

"But guys," I started crying. All of a sudden, I was struck with fright and anxiety, "What bothers me the most, besides my insecurities is Anthony. He's a lunatic and a criminal. Even though he's in jail right now...."

"Back up!" shouted Malova, "When did he get locked up?"

"Two weeks ago. He called me from Avenal to come and bail him out."

"I know you didn't...." Malova placed her hands on her hips.

"Down, girl!" Varsha held up her hand to stop Malova from going off the deep end. "She didn't bail him out."

"No I didn't. I didn't have a desire to go and rescue him. It serves him right for getting all of those innocent people killed. Even though there were some not so innocent people in that club, that still doesn't give him the right to play executioner. He's so notorious that he was on Long Beach's Most Wanted."

"I remember that segment," said Mike, "They were talking about Bookie Nole, that dude that used to slang dope for Anthony."

"That's the one! They also talked about Derrick Love, Shawn Deiter and Clair Vice -- they all used to work for Anthony, and they are all dead because they were all in the club that night. Everyone suspects that Anthony did it, but they didn't have enough evidence to convict him. Even though he got caught, he will either figure out some way to get bail and then get off on the charges or just break out of jail and be a loser on the run. The point of me even going into all that is because he's put a threat on Wil's life."

Malova stood up and starting pacing. She started shaking her head, while her hand was on her hip. When she does this, she often says things that are thought provoking. "First off, Wil doesn't come off as a punk by any means. Based off what you told us at the beginning of this conversation, William Masterton can handle his own. I mean, he held this dude up in mid air choking him."

"You do have a point. He did handle Anthony quite well at my house. Even after Anthony left, you could tell that he would have killed him had I not stepped in."

"He also walked in on Anthony totally disrespecting you, and it set him off. Any good man would have gotten mad to see anyone treat someone they care about like that."

"The point is that Wil can handle his own. And if you're questioning if Wil is as crazy as Anthony, then get that thought out of your head now. Anthony and Wil are two different people. I'd bet on Wil any day to not only defend your honor, but be there for you no matter what; to the death if need be. What he did for you that day was demonstrating his commitment, whether it's friendship or more. I'm putting my money on Wil wanting to be with you just as much as you want to be with him." said Greg.

"Finally, don't worry about it. Bottom line is, if Anthony dreams of hurting you in any kind of way, to include hurting Wil, he'd have to get through all of us first." said Mike.

"Yeah, Courtni, we're here for you, always. That's never going to change. We're a team, remember?" asked Varsha.

They all offered me a group hug. I'm so blessed to have the friends that I have in my life. After everyone ate, we started drinking and singing karaoke. It's always fun to be around them, but it's even better when karaoke is involved.

The emails and IMs never stopped. Anthony was still silent and hopefully rotting in his jail cell. A couple of days after I had my friends over, Wil emailed me stating he had to stay even longer. Though I understood, but the suspense was still killing me. I didn't want to tell him how I felt over the phone, but I really didn't want to wait another month either. Things happen for a reason, I told myself. I'm now glad I waited.

I took a Sunday afternoon to go and sit down on the beach. Before I chose my spot, I looked over at their pier and said to myself, this is where it all began. I still can't believe that Malova embarrassed me like that. I wasn't trying to meet anyone. Regret, disappointment and embarrassment were the only occupied my thoughts. Who knew that Wil would be so different? Who knew that he would actually be a gentleman?

Why would he be interested in me? I'm not worthy of a man like him.

I sat down in the sand, staring out into the ocean. *How come I'm not worthy?* I'm a good woman. All I need is a good man that will lift me up. I'm afraid though. Afraid that he won't see me as worthy. Or, this may be one elaborate show to ensnare me. Once he feels comfortable, he could show his true colors; he could be worse than Anthony! My heart says he not, and for once my brain is agreeing with my heart. His patience, kindness and his humbleness illuminate from him. I can feel his presence, even though he's miles away. We can talk about everything and laugh about nothing. It's amazing that I've allowed myself to miss out on the wonders of a true connection. I thought I had a connection with all of the men I dated. It was a connection that should have never been bonded in the first place. This is different, and though I am still afraid of being hurt, I feel that Wil is worth the possible risk. For all I know, it may be the best relationship decision I've made ever.

Two weeks after my emotional journey at the beach, my friends came over for a barbeque cook out. We were all eating, laughing and drinking our hearts content. Even over the loud music, Malova could hear the phone ring. I looked over and saw Malova laughing and smiling. That was a good sign of it not being Anthony calling. I was curious to find out who she was speaking to, so I went into my bedroom to grab the phone.

"I'm glad that you're father is doing better. I'm still surprised that you remember me." She's talking to Wil. No wonder she was all smiling and cheesing. I'm sure she's marveling in the fact that she hooked us up. Malova gloats like that.

"How can I forget the woman that brought Courtni and I together? Besides, it's nice to hear your voice again." It's good to hear your voice. Technology is wonderful but give me the telephone any day, especially when it comes to you."

"Aw, you flatter me. You're family will continue to be in my prayers. Now, before my man get's jealous I had better call Courtni to the phone."

"I already got the phone, thank you."

"Dang that was quick. I didn't even get the chance to bellow your name. You got some telephony thing going or something?"

"Hang up the phone before I tell Mike on you."

"You didn't even have to go there. You know he'll make me sleep on the couch. Anyway, Wil, it was nice talking to you. I'll leave you to your lady."

I heard the phone click. Finally, I can get to my conversation in peace. "Hey there. How are things going down south?"

"Pretty good. My father is getting better, and we're all happy about that. Just to be on the safe side, he's signed all of his businesses over to me. That means I own all the businesses on the Pier, La Bonita, The Sandals Suites Hotel downtown and the Masterton Estates -- which is down the street from your house."

"That gigantic house was owned by your father?"

"Yep, he used it as a winter home, mostly and when he had to be up here to see to personal things with the business located here. The old guy decided I was ready to take responsibility for them. I'm kind of nervous about it, but God has a plan that I willingly follow. I think the most exciting part about all this for me is having a private jet with a small air field twenty minutes outside of town."

"That's wonderful. Seems like you got a full plate now."

"It appears that way, but my plate is never too full for you. Speaking of you, I know you're friends are over, and I don't want to interrupt what you all are doing…"

"It's okay; and you know they don't mind. Besides, it's really good to hear you voice. I've been longing to hear you"

"Wow. I am flattered and relieved that I'm not the only one with those feelings."

"Are you calling to tell me that you're going to have to stay longer? If so, then I'd like to tell you some things that have been on my mind. I'd rather say it in person, but a phone conversation will suffice."

"I still have some final arrangement to take care of here, but I can't wait a couple of more weeks to see you. I miss you Courtni. I know we talk through instant messenger, but it's nothing like looking at you."

"I miss you too."

"Well, I'm going to take advantage of having a private jet. If you don't mind, I'd love to have a limo to pick you up and bring you to the air field. I'll have the jet fueled up, and we can spend some true alone time together. Sure they'll be a flight attendant, but outside of that it will be me and you, in person. What do you say?"

"Like I'm really going to say no; I'll be ready in thirty minutes. "

"You got some time. It'll take me four hours to get there."

"Great. I'll see you then."

I slowly placed the phone on the receiver. Now I'm really afraid. Most rich men feel that they can do whatever it is they choose and the women should stand by and take it. As long as the charge cards don't run out, the women are supposed to be quiet. I've seen it so many times as a photographer. Not all photo shoots are done in a studio, so I get to see how some people live. Then again, I dated a broke bastard that treated me like scum, and I didn't even get paid. There was something inside of me that was trying to talk myself out of telling Wil I'm ready to take the next step. Every time that feeling rises, my heart wins out, and I find something to destroy that feeling or the doubt is removed. And besides, I'm going on a jet ride and need to get ready. This is unbelievable! While marveling in my thoughts, I heard a fast busy signal in the other room. I ran out my bedroom and everyone was crowded by the speaker phone in the foyer.

"What are you all doing?" placing my hand on my hips.

"He owns an air field and a jet?" asked Mike.

"That big-ass house sitting at the edge of your block is called the Masterton Estates, or should I say the William Masterton Estates?" asked Varsha.

"That dude is fire! For real, girl; you set! A good man with money? You cannot ask for anything more." said Malova.

"Hold on, ya'll. Let's not forget he has all his father's businesses. All I want to know is can I get a hook up with a room at the Sandals?" asked Greg.

"The monetary items are perks, but all I want is the man behind the perks."

Varsha walked over to me, and placed her hand on my shoulder. "Well I hear you girl. This is your time to tell him. Are you ready?"

"Ready as I'm going to get."

"You won't be sorry. Just have faith. We'll vamp out so you can properly get ready. I mean, you gotta' look fly for your scenic jet ride." said Varsha.

"Alright, good people. Thanks for understanding and the good food. Mike, you're a beast on that grill!"

"Yeah, I try to do what I can so when I can do it." Mike replied.

"I'm so thankful for all of you. I can't and don't want to imagine my life without you. If I don't tell you enough, know that you all mean the world to me."

"Girl, we know we got you. Go ahead and get ready. I want a full report after the date is over." replied Malova.

After I walked them out, I started focusing on getting ready. This is the most exciting thing since I went to the Ace of Base concert (I know – that really shows my age, but they were a great band)!

Once Wil arrived at my house, his limo took us to the air field where we boarded his private jet. It was nice! Cozy, comfortable and loaded with food and beverages. He took me to the Mississippi Opera, which is located in Jackson. We saw "Carmen", which was an amazing show, even though the production was in French. Considering I own the movie with Dorothy Dandridge, I pretty much knew what was going on. After the opera, we went to a local steak house for dinner and talked for hours. Before I knew it, it was 2 A.M., We stayed overnight at a hotel that was above the steakhouse. Wil respected my privacy and slept in a different room. A part of me was bummed because I wanted him to stay with me, but it was best in the end. My attraction to him has grown since the day we met. I know he doesn't believe in sex before marriage, and I know me. I would have tested the waters. Great things happen and are experienced over time. Waiting, though difficult, will prove to have been worth it. Based off his body structure and how incredible he looks in jeans, I'm confident that I won't be disappointed. But thinking about how he would look out of his jeans – I need to put my mind somewhere else!

We checked out at 9 A.M. and boarded his jet. While watching the soft clouds go by, Wil grabbed my hand.

"Did you have a good time?" he asked.

"I did. It was much needed time away."

"That's good. Sorry we were out so late. I planned on having you back home yesterday."

"It's okay. I didn't have anything planned. The only thing I may do is pay some bills and talk on the phone with the gang."

"Your life seems so simple and fun. Mine seems complicated and not as much fun as I would want it to be."

"I don't know about all that, but why don't you think your life isn't fun? You have everything you want and probably more. What else is there?"

"Not everything. I don't have you, Courtni."

"Yes, you do, in a way. I'm open for it being more than what we have today."

"So, have you thought about what I asked before I left?"

"Yes, I have. I've done more thinking than I care to admit while you've been gone. I've decided that I am not going to play a victim to my past relationship with Anthony. I am ready to move on with life and love. I'm ready to move on with you."

His facial expression changed. He looked shocked as if he had just seen a ghost. I guess he was prepared in case I said no. I can't say that I blame him, considering all the fighting, I've done against falling for him. Wil stared at me with those dark brown eyes, as if he wanted to kiss me. I leaned over for that kiss, but was interrupted by turbulence, as the plane was landing. After leaving the plane, we got back into his limo and his driver took me home. Wil walked me to my front door. As I turned the lock to open it, Wil grabbed my hand.

"Tonight has been an essence to me." said Wil.

"Same here. I really enjoyed myself and spending time with you. Are you going back to Mississippi soon?"

"I am tonight because I have to get some more stuff, but I'll be back the day after tomorrow in the afternoon. I have to get ready for my big move into the estate."

"At least we'll be closer. You could literally walk down the street to my house."

"This is true. You could walk up to me, yourself, ya know?"

"You don't know what you are asking for. I'll be at your house every other day with that kind of invitation."

"I welcome your presence."

"So I guess this is where a new chapter begins with us, right?"

"Yep. I don't think you'll be disappointed."

"I know I won't."

"I'll call you in the morning."

"Okay."

We stared into each other's eyes. I was thinking to myself, *here we go again.* I want his lips on mine so bad. The message is his eyes were clear. He felt the same way, but the question was who was going to make the first move. Then like a tidal wave rushing the beach, he took me into his arms and kissed me with complete passion. His lips were everything I had imagined and more. His tongue was smooth and gentle -- caressing mine. Oh, how I wanted this kiss to last forever. In my heart it did, because our first kiss was the comfort of knowing he was truly mine.

Chapter Six

My relationship with Wil is like a dream come true. I wake up every morning praying that this part of my life continues to be a reality. It's so amazing to be with a man that actually cherishes me. He actually spends time with me, talks to me like a person, and is genuinely concerned with my wants and desires. It has been quite a challenge to avoid being intimate with him, but Wil's kisses and tender touch has been more than satisfactory. We have yet to have a major argument, and if we disagree on anything, we actually talk it out and come to a mutual understanding. I have never had this type of relationship, and I must say that I am having the best time of my life.

Wil left me a voicemail saying that he has a surprise for me but refuses to tell me what it is. I didn't have any clients to shoot today, so I decided to go shopping with Malova and Varsha. After we maxed out all of our credit cards, we stopped at The Red Dragon for lunch. Our conversations, as always, were wild and crazy. Varsha talked about her and Greg's wedding plans. They couldn't decide if they were going to have a spring or fall wedding. All Varsha knew is that her dress was going to be a custom made gown. She wanted her gown to mimic Juliet in Shakespeare's Romeo and Juliet play. It felt really good to know that she was elated about her future with Greg. Malova was happy as well, but also frustrated due to Mike's hesitation in proposing to her. One of the many great things about Mike is that he believes that once you get married – it's forever. His parents have been married for fifty-five years and they still hug and kiss each other. I know he loves, but what she doesn't understand is that he wants to make sure everything is right with their future. I love Malova but she does lack in the patience department. If things are done when she wants them done, you can expect to hear a lot of nagging. To Malova's point, he is dragging his feet a bit. It's not like they are like Wil and me

– in the beginning stages of a relationship. There's only so much "pre-planning" you can do to ensure the right time, place and person. I personally feel that they are meant to be and really should stop fighting each other on this issue. When I expressed that to Malova, she frowned and threw her fortune cookie at me. We all had a really good laugh out of that. When it was my time for interrogation, I just smiled and expressed how wonderful things were in my relationship. For them it was an astonishment that I didn't have anything negative to stay or any secrets to hide. No more black eyes, busted lip or swollen insides from harsh sexual encounters. It felt good to sit at the table with my friends and tell them for the first time ever, "I have an exceptional man in my life."

After lunch with the girls, Wil called me to let me know he was going to pick me up around 7 P.M. I was thrilled about my surprise – even though I had no clue what is was. When I arrived at home I jumped in the shower. After washing my hair and applying Bath and Body Cherry Blossom lotion, it was 6 P.M. -- I had a little time to kill. I decided to switch on the TV. While flipping through the channels, Anthony's face caught my eye, so I changed the channel back to see what was going on. The anchorman was reporting that he had broken out of jail, and they had all of the officers that were on duty during the break in custody. I stared at the TV with fear and annoyance. I hadn't heard from him since the day he called begging me to get bail money. I really wanted it to stay that way, but I figured that would be asking too much.

I decided to cut the TV off, as it was depressing me. I got up and went to pick out what I was going to wear. I decided to go with the red, sexy spaghetti strap halter dress. It was thirty-two inches in length, so it was short, but not too short. As soon as I put my shoes on, I heard the doorbell ring. I opened it and saw Daidus and some other guy at the door. I could already tell this wasn't going to be a congenial conversation. Whenever Daidus is around, trouble is either with him, or it follows him. From the looks of the gentleman that he was with, trouble was standing right beside him. Daidus companion was a 5'9", slender, fair skinned with freckles. His red hair stood up through the Doo-rag that was tied around his head. His gaze was extremely disturbing. I could contemplate what he was thinking but when I tried, I became ill to my stomach. Him standing there and running his tongue across three of his teeth which were plated in gold didn't make me feel better either.

"What do you want, Daidus?" I asked.

"Have you seen Tone?" asked Daidus.

"Now you know the answer to that question, Daidus!"

"I thought he might have come by here, since he broke out of prison."

"I don't know why you would think that. I'm sure your sister told you that I have a man in my life, and it's not Anthony!"

"Look bitch," said the other guy. I looked at him and thought to myself, no you didn't just call me a bitch. "I don't care about who you with. Anthony owes me money and I am here to collect!"

"How dare you disrespect my home, Daidus!" I started turning beet red with anger.

"Courtni, you know it's not like that...."

"Yes it is like that! Like I said bitch -- according to Anthony's letter to Daidus, he was going to leave my money with you. Now, when Slippin' Sim Jimma is owed money, I expect to collect!"

"Like I told you, whatever the hell your name is there's no money here for you! Not that it's any of your business, but I have not talked to Anthony in over a year, and I'd like to keep it that way."

"You're a lying ass hoe!" He pulled a gun from his back pocket and pointed it to my face. Daidus' eyes bucked and he tried to grab the gun. The gangster wanna-be smacked

Daidus in the back of his head and Daidus buckled to the floor. The gun was pointed towards Daidus now. I was too angry to be scared but started to cry nonetheless. I couldn't believe this was happening on my anniversary. I was so glad that Wil wasn't here yet. I looked at the clock and noticed it was 6:34P.M. I started praying God, please remove these fools from my doorstep before Wil shows up.

"What did you hit me for Jimma?" asked Daidus while he was bleeding on my porch.

"You dumb mutha'fucka! You grabbed my piece! Don't nobody grab my piece!"

"You promised me you wouldn't use any violence! Courtni is my family, man! If she says that Tone ain't sent no money, then he ain't sent no money here man! He lied to both of us!"

"Since she's your family, it would make sense for you to lie for her. You think you two can pull something here? I know my money is here, and I am going to collect it one way or another!"

"Look, Jimma, Jimmy, Jo-Jo, whatever your name is!" I was crying uncontrollably at this point, "Daidus isn't lying and neither am I. I don't know you, so I would have no reason to lie. There's nothing for you here. I don't know why Anthony told you there would be money here. Please leave and let Daidus stay here with me. He needs medical attention."

"I don't care what he needs. I am not leaving here without my money." He took his gun and slapped me across the face with it. As I started falling to the ground, he also managed to push me aside to get into the house.

As I sat there and held my face, I could hear several things breaking in the house. I thought to myself, I'm not even with Anthony anymore, and I'm still getting beat up. I looked over at Daidus, and I saw that he wasn't breathing. I crawled to him and started shaking him. His body seemed lifeless. I started sobbing more. Jimma was screaming and continued throwing things around. This odd feeling of peace and satisfaction came over me. Even though he was trashing my house, I was still happy that he was being proven wrong.

Jimma came out of the back room, pulling his hair and crossing his eyes. He had the gun resting on his right ear. I attempted to smile but felt myself getting really light headed. He turned the gun towards me. I started shaking and crying again.

"Where is it!" yelled Jimma.

"I told you it wasn't here. I don't know why Anthony lied to you, but he did."

"Freeze!" A police officer showed up at the door. It was strange because I didn't hear the sirens. "Put the gun down and place your hand behind your head."

"I ain't doing nothing, pig!" Jimma took the gun off of me and pointed it at the officer. "Someone is going to tell me where my money is, or everyone up in here is going to DIE!"

"I said put the gun down and place your hands behind your head!"

"Fuck you -- you ain't gon' shoot!"

I heard a loud pop and Jimma crashed to the floor holding his knee. More police officers rushed in to pick him up and cuff him. A paramedic went over to Daidus to check him over. He still wasn't breathing. Even though I couldn't stand Daidus on account of his lifestyle, he was still like a brother to me -- I didn't want him to die.

"Courtni, are you all right?" Wil rushed in the door. I was so happy to see him and even happier that he hadn't come sooner. I wrapped my arms around him and held him tightly.

"I'm okay. My head hurts a little."

"We need to get you to the hospital then."

"No! We have plans!"

"We can pick up our plans later. Right now you need to get checked out."

The paramedic began a series of questions to determine the extent of my injuries. Though I wasn't in the mood to cooperate with then, I answered their questions – with quick and short phrases. I was determined not to spend my anniversary in a hospital or an ER. After they checked me over, I stood up and fell to the ground. When I regained consciousness, I woke up and saw that I was rushed to LB Memorial Hospital. To me, it was a waste. The doctor said I had a mild concussion. His orders were for me to stay off my feet, apply ice to my head and take Naproxen 1000 mg tablets once every six hours – as needed for pain. Not trying to sound ungrateful or anything, but I didn't need to spend $200 in the ER for that diagnosis. I could have bought more film or something with that money.

As I waited to be discharged, Wil came into the room with my coat. It was now 11:50P.M. , and our evening was almost over. Needless to say I was not jovial, and it didn't help that Wil didn't seem to share my disappointment.

"The doctor told me you're almost ready to go." said Wil.

"I didn't want to be here in the first place. I told you I was fine."

"When you fell on your butt you didn't look fine."

"Yeah, whatever," I started laughing. It even hurt to laugh at that point, but I didn't care because I was with Wil. "Any word on Daidus?"

"He's recovering and going back to jail. I overheard an officer say he has a bunch of outstanding warrants, and he hasn't visited his parole officer in two months."

"That's Daidus for you. What about Jimma?"

"He's been patched up and is on his way to Lompoc County. They are going to see if they can use him to find Anthony. I heard he escaped from prison."

"Don't remind me; that's why Jimma was at my house."

"He hasn't contacted you, has he?"

"No, not since he called to get me to bail him out of jail."

"Why did he send Jimma to your house?"

"Now that I think about it, what better way to get revenge on me?"

"Not trying to say that I don't believe you, but what's your logic behind that?"

"I dump him; he knows I'm dating you; I refused to bail him out, and I blocked my phone from receiving collect calls. Anthony could not care less that I broke up with him, but to him, it's the principle of me embarrassing him. Since he can't do it himself because he's on the run, he sent a messenger of sorts to rough me up on his behalf."

"I follow you, but why lie to this Jimma guy?"

"Easy, most of his people liked me, even though the feeling was not mutual. Unless he would have paid any of them butt loads of money, they wouldn't touch me. Anthony is a money hoarder, so he wasn't trying to pay anyone to come after me. It's easier and cheaper to lie."

"That man is twisted."

"That's putting it nicely. You know, I don't want to talk about him anymore. Let's go to better subjects like, what was my surprise?"

"Well, this isn't the way I wanted to give it to you, but because of today's events I want to do this before midnight."

He reached into his back pocket and pulled out a small black box. The first thing that came to mind was I'm getting a marriage proposal in a hospital bed. Then my thoughts changed to, is he crazy? We've only been together for a year, and he's already asking me to marry him? Something must be wrong. He got down on his knees, and as he started opening the box, I got really scared. I can't say yes to a marriage proposal right now. The box completely opened and I was relieved. It wasn't a ring -- it was a key.

"I want you to move in with me." he said.

"Wow, this is a different surprise." I know this may sound weird but a small part of me was disappointed that it wasn't a ring. "I have to admit, I am flattered, but I am not so sure if I can accept this."

"Why not?"

"Because I think living with someone before marriage is wrong."

"You know, I agree with you, but if it makes you feel any better, I want it to be more like a roommate situation."

"What does that mean, exactly?"

"Well, we would live in the same house but in different sections. My room is in the east wing, and you can either take the central wing or the west wing. You can contribute to utilities and may decorate your wing any way you would like."

"Wil, you don't need a roommate so you are going to have to do better than that."

"Alright – you got me on that one. Look, I think about tonight and things you have gone through with Anthony – things that maybe yet to come because he's broken out of jail. Call me old fashioned but I want to protect you. Sure I can come over your house everyday, but I want to be able to see you when I wake up in the morning and when I go to bed at night. I want twenty-four hours of Courtni Taylor and the Masterton Mansion."

"So what -- we're going to be like Beauty and the Beast or something?"

"You're funny," he started laughing, but I wasn't.
I had lived in my house ever since we moved to Long Beach. My mom died there, which in a funny way is why I held on to the house. I thought in a way I could hold on to her. "It's no

pressure. If you don't want to move in, that's fine. You still can keep the key -- come over anytime you like. Since I want twenty-four hours of Courtni Taylor, it's only fair that you are granted exclusive access to William Masterton."

"You are so cute," I couldn't help but laugh at him. In between the chuckles my heart was melting. By no means have I ever had true protection in a relationship before. Not only does Wil want to protect me physically, but he has been protecting my heart from the moment of our first date. "I appreciate your offer and all you are trying to do. Forgive me, but I cannot see myself moving in with you before we're married. Maybe I'll change my mind one day, but it won't be today."

"I understand and respect your decision."

"I will accept the key though."

He got off his knees and kissed me. I wrapped my arms around him and heard a whisper. I wasn't sure what he said, but it sounded like *I love you*. I looked at him with concern and asked...

"What did you say?"

"I said I love you." My heart started beating more rapidly. At this rate, I may need to stay in the hospital.

"You've never said that before."

"That was because I wasn't sure. I'm not the type of person that uses that phrase loosely. Love is an amazing, prevailing gift that should never be misused. Our society has forgotten the true meaning of love, but I haven't. If you don't feel that same way yet--"

"I do," It seemed like in that very moment everything was right in my life. Even though the ending of the day had turned tragic, this moment made it all worthwhile. "I've felt this way for quite some time, but I was too afraid to tell you. The last man I loved – that I thought I loved...well....you see the type of man he turned out to be."

"And you should know by now that I am a man and not some little boy. I respect you as a woman -- especially as my lady. I hope you know I would never hurt you."

"I know you wouldn't."

"Never be afraid to tell me anything. To keep this good thing going, communication is important. Like I told you before, if we can't talk, then we don't have anything worth holding on to."

"You don't have to worry about that. We got something worth holding."

"Let's get you home, baby."

Chapter Seven

My relationship with Wil is like no other I've been in before. Never in my life could I have said that I am in the perfect partnership with a man. We have yet to have an argument, and if we have opposing issues we agree to disagree. He respects my mind as well as my body. Even though both of our businesses have grown respectively, we still manage to balance our love quite effectively. I am not use to having this much stability in my life – I am not complaining though. Lately, we have had many conversations around me moving in to his place. The thought was wearing on me more and more. He wasn't pressuring me, but it seemed like every time I spent the night over his house, he would ask me to stay. Some morning it's hard to get up and go home. I hold fast to my beliefs, but it wears on me daily.

It's mid January and I have a winter shoot with some rising celebrities. I was leaving Wil's house when my sister Diedra called. She was having some man problems, and she always looks to me for advice. I never understood why though. Heck, just recently I could get a handle on my love life. She's dating this guy that she met at a Subway restaurant. He's been very mysterious in what he does for a living – among other things. Most of the time I listen and let her make her own decisions. Today I decided to take the lead as n older sister.

"Let him go about his business," I said, "You deserve so much more."

"Courtni, you've never told me to leave a guy alone." It was obvious she was shocked. I just hope that she take my advice when this is all over.

"Yeah well your sister has learned some valuable lessons and trust me hon – if I can save you from the road I went down I will do it in a heartbeat."

"He's not as bad as Anthony!"

"From what you have told me, he screams Anthony clone! It's not clear what his base of income is, when you question him he raises his voice at you and after he gets some he's up..."

"That's because he has to work early."

"Dee, don't be stupid. Open your eyes and pay attention to the signs. You're a smart girl and smart girls don't date dumb hustling men."

"Yeah I guess you're right. I'm tired of jumping from man to man though."

"You're young. This is the time to do it. Also, this let's you know who's the one for you and who's not. Enjoy these moments, Dee. You'll never have them again."

"Do you miss being single Courtni?"

"Not by a long shot!"

"Well why it is six months later, and you have yet to move in with Wil? The two of you have been together for a little over two years now."

"I just don't believe that people should move in together before they get married."

"Gracious chick you sound like mom! We live in a different time. There's nothing wrong with it. Besides, the house is so big that you two could technically sleep in different sections of the house."

"Yeah you're right and I have been thinking about it..."

"Stop thinking about it and take the plunge."

"I can't believe my little sister is giving me advice."

"Yeah it feels good too. Besides, it will allow me to not having to re-new my lease at my crappy apartment."

"Oh so the truth comes out!"

"That's not the main reason. I don't know what it is about William Masterton but when I think of you two, I see a real future. You two were meant to be and nothing will separate the two of you."

"I hope you're right Dee."

"This time, I know I am right." I heard my phone beep. I pulled it away from my ear, and I saw it was Wil.

"Well Dee, I'm going to get off of here. This is Wil calling."

"Okay sis! You better tell him you're moving in."

"Yeah aight! Bye!" I pressed the button on my phone to answer Wil's call. I automatically started grinning. "Hey honey."

"Hey yourself. What you doing?"

"Nothing much. I just got off the phone with Diedra. I was attempting to give her advice about the latest loser she was dating, but she ended up schooling me on some things."

"Yeah, like what?"

"Like me moving in to your place."

"Don't play! That's a battle I think I have finally given up on so don't mess with my emotions."

"I'm serious. She brought up some good points, and I am willing to put my thoughts on the subject aside. I am interested in seeing if my sister is right."

"Is she the only reason why you're going to move in?"

"Of course not dearest. Besides the fact of loving you and stuff, I just want to be more close to you. Every time I spend the night it's sometimes painful because I know I have to get up and go home the next day."

"Now you know how I feel when you're not coming back."

"I always come back to you – I never leave."

"You're being sarcastic."

"I know, and I know what you mean. I want to give it a shot if it's all right with you."

"You know it's all right with me. What are you going to do with the house?"

"Well Dee has already staked her claim on it. It's good timing for her because I know she's unhappy where she's staying. At least she'll have the opportunity to own a home and not have to worry about landlord scum."

"So true. So when are you moving your stuff in?"

"There's no time like the present. I'll start tonight."

"Don't worry about it. I'll get some movers to get your things out. So things won't be uncomfortable I'll have your thing set up in the West Wing of the house. You'll have your own living space."

"That's fine. At least I won't have to walk so far to get in my own bed."

"Who said you were getting in your own bed?"

"Oh behave Mr. Masterton..."

Within a month's time, I moved all my stuff out of my mom's house and assisted Diedra with moving her stuff in. It was hard to let it go, but if Wil and I have a future together, I know he wouldn't give up his mansion to stay in a four bedroom, ranch style home (I know I wouldn't). I thought that us living in different wings of the mansion would lessen the sexual tension. Wil was right about me never leaving his room. I only went to the West Wing to change clothes or develop pictures from work the previous day. The more he took me into his bed (to cuddle and sleep that is), the more I wanted him pressed inside me. Since it's so close to Valentine's Day, I'm hoping he'll negotiate by breaking his rule and break me off a little' something. Lord, I know that's wrong to think that way, but I am beyond horny. I respected that my man was a virgin, and he wanted to wait until he was married. When I lay next to him some nights, all I feel is brown, smooth and beautiful skin against mine. I try not to caress lower than I should but my hands slip on occasion (Okay it's intentional – I'm guilty). To feel him bulge through his boxers takes me to a place that leaves me shivering and moist. Some mornings when he's awake before me, he sneaks off in the shower. When I open my eyes , the vision that awaits me is my man standing butt naked in the shower. I can see the drops of water running down the curves of his body. The sight alone leaves me drooling and my wetness running down my thighs. The smell of my pre-orgasm elevates my hormones; leaving my nipples throbbing and the rest of my body shivering. Wil's shape is perfect and all his curves are placed with precision. He could make any woman weak in the knees.

The day of Cupid was finally upon us. Normally, I would cringe at the thought of Valentine's Day but these past few years I have looked forward to it. As always, Wil had a marvelous day planned for us. We had gone to the zoo, had lunch at La Bonita, and went shopping. Later in the evening he had his maid cook a sublime dinner prepared for is. The menu consisted of broccoli sweet onion and Georgia Pecan salad, cherry glazed carrots and hamburger steak with strawberry sauce. The dessert of the evening was here's My Heart Shortcake – a yellow cake with various berries and lemon ice mixed in. It was the best Valentine's meal I'd ever had. After the delicious meal, Wil grabbed my hands and led me upstairs. The lights were low; his bed was made with black satin sheets, and there were red and white rose petals all over. Wil sat me on the bed and undressed, leaving nothing but black satin boxers. I was trying my best not to get wet just by looking at him.

"Honey, what is all this? And why are you teasing me with those boxers?" I asked.
"You'll see. Just relax," he said.

He went over to the surround sound stereo, and turned on "Truly, Madly, Deeply" by Savage Gardens. Wil took me into his arms and kissed me passionately. His hands traveled down the small of my back and he gently grabbed my ass. I giggled a little and then he started laughing as well. He got down on one knee and grabbed a black ring box from underneath the bed. My eyes widened with excitement, because he was about to ask the question I had been waiting to hear.

"Courtni, I love you, and I want to be with you for the rest of my life. Now, when I ask you this, and you respond, be sure because this is forever. I believe in marriage vows, and I hold them in high regard -- just as God does. I'm yours -- forever. Even beyond the grave, I will be with you and will love you. Will you marry me?"

"I can't believe this," I started crying. I couldn't help it. At this point, I could barely speak. "I would have never thought I could love anymore the way I love you. You have no idea how long I have waited for you to ask. Yes, I will marry you."

We both smothered each other with hugs and kisses. Soon after we sat down on the bed and started discussing plans.

"So, you have a date in mind?" he asked.

"No, but I would like to do a Fall wedding. You know, just to be a little different. Most people get married in the spring and summer."

"That's true, but you know that only gives us six months to prepare."

"I'm okay with as long as you are."

"Sure. You just tell me where and what time to show up. That's all the man is required to do anyways. All I ask is that we are married in a church, and the reception is here at the house. With all this space, it's pointless to rent a hall somewhere."

"Agreed. The mansion is the absolute best place for me to have my bachelorette party. I'm thinking more towards the end of July."

"You want a stripper, don't you?"

"Of course I do! Mainly, for my girlfriends though. Don't you want one?"

"Yeah, but I'm not worried about that right now. I'd rather strip you instead."

"You'd rather what?"

"You heard me."

"That's not nice!"

"It can be."

"No because that's how stuff gets started. We've been good all this time, so as far as I am concerned, we can wait until the wedding night. I'll admit it's been difficult, but we've managed."

"Oh, don't worry. I won't let it go too far. Besides, if you get too carried away, I can always stop you. Now, come here."

He grabbed me and kissed me with desire. My body started shaking because I wanted him so badly. I felt tortured. I started to moisten on the crotch of my panties. His soft, warm lips went down to my neck, kissing me with absolute passion. His arms were wrapped around me, and his hands guided the way to pure ecstasy. While easing down to the floor, Wil climbed on top of me and started kissing my breast. While savoring one of my hardened nipples in his mouth, one hand was holding mine and the other was caressing my thighs. He undressed me slowly. His lips explored every part of me. I rendered myself helpless. All I could do was roll my eyes in the back of my head and moan. He picked me up and placed me on the bed. Wil backed away slowly and took off his boxers. I've never met or seen a man that possessed that much power. I was speechless…all I could do was stare. It was the most amazing thing I'd ever witnessed. While my eyes still gazed upon him, he lowered his head and started to kiss my inner thighs. I had never been kissed there before and the feeling was unreal. He came up to my navel and licked the inside of it, which tickled a little, but I didn't mind. After my slight giggle, Wil looked at me and smiled. Our eyes met and I could see what I had in him was genuine. I finally had someone that was willing to do anything for me. After that he attacked my warm, wet love. I screamed a romantic cry and trembled. The feeling was like a burst of energy that ran through me. Wil lavished me with his tongue until I came. He lifted his head and I watched him lick my wetness. His look was that of satisfaction. My cum was a warm refreshment for his mouth. After swirling his tongue around his lips for the last drop of my love, he came up and slowly licked my nipples. I grabbed the back of his head and moaned with satisfaction. He stopped, grabbed the back of my hair and gently pulled it. While staring into my eyes he whispered," I love you."

We both fell asleep in each other's arms. My dreams were filled with pleasantries of a new life that I was about to embark upon with Wil. I woke up the next morning, with the sun shining brightly through the bedroom window. There was a Blue Jay resting on a branch just outside the window. I thought to myself, Is this a dream? This can't really be my life, can it? I rolled over and saw Wil sleeping. I crawled out of bed and went to my bedroom for a little privacy. I couldn't wait to tell Malova I was getting married.

"Girlfriend, I'm engaged!"
"Are you really?" asked Malova in amazement.
"Yes!"
"Congratulations."
"Thank you."
"So, how did he ask?"
"Now, you know I am not a fan of kiss and tell, but I will say that we had a night I'll never forget."
"Ya'll did it, didn't you?"
"No, we didn't do it, but don't think I didn't want to."
"Girl I know you wanted to tap that. Hell, I was hoping that he would cave in one of these days and break you off like you need to be."
"Well I'm going to have to wait for the Full Monte. I did get a little sampler platter though. After he proposed and I accepted, we had intense foreplay until we both passed out."

"Oh, you are so nasty! How was he girl? I want a full report over lunch. Can I call Varsha and give her the scoop? She'll be shocked."

"Okay you do that. But before you go, will you be my matron of honor?"

"Now you know that was automatic. You wasted time asking the question."

"You are so cocky at times!"

"It's all good though because what would life be without cocky old me." We both started laughing. I felt so lifted. My body was glowing with radiance and excitement, "Courtni, I am truly happy for you. We'll do lunch at twelve-thirty."

"No problem."

As I was hanging up the phone, I felt footsteps behind me. I turned around and it was Wil putting his arms around me holding me tightly.

"Good morning, my queen. How did you sleep?"

"Hey. Last night was the best sleep I've had in years."

"That makes two of us then. I really enjoyed tasting you. It was absolutely wonderful."

"It was for me too. That was the first time a man has ever placed all his focus on pleasing me."

"When you're pleased, so am I. It's the only way. I heard you talking to Malova. You couldn't wait until we had a proper social gathering?"

"What can I say? She's my best friend. I had to tell her."

"It's understood."

"Well I'd better get up. Next thing you know, it will be twelve-thirty. I'll see you when I get back."

"I have to make a short stop at La Bonita. It seems that some of my staff has been slinging their drugs behind my restaurant. I'm going to do some terminations, performance reviews plus conduct interviews. The last time I had a hiring spree, there were several candidates that were strong, but not selected."

"Probably some of Anthony's friends."

"Who knows? I'm nothing like Max Campbell. Have I ever told you the story of Max Campbell?"

"No, sweetie, you haven't."

"Well, he used to be the manager before my father allowed me to take over. Max would allow any and everything to go on in the restaurant. I don't see why Father let him run that place for as long as he did. I only want classy people and classy employees in my establishment. Not hookers, pimps, and broke salesmen wanting to be the next Donald Trump. If they want to get their freelance on, then they need to go up the street somewhere."

"I understand where you're coming from, but what if that broke salesman has money to spend in your restaurant?"

"Then that's fine. He can spend it. I have a problem when you are trying to solicit your Amway products in between drinks."

"Alright. I follow now. Well, I'd better get dressed. I'll see you when you get back then."

"I love you, Courtni."

"I love you too.

At twelve-forty, my friends and I were sitting down at Utsukushii's, a popular Japanese cuisine restaurant, which coincidentally means beautiful in Japanese.

"Courtni Renee Taylor getting married," said Varsha, "I just can't believe it."

"When's the wedding?" asked Mike.

"Sometime in October -- probably at the end."

"That's wonderful!" exclaimed Greg.

"Enough with that crap. I want the particulars of last night's event after the proposal. What color were the drawers?" said Malova.

"That would be disclosing way too much information. I can't deny that it was a marvelous experience. Hell, I think it's better than sex."

"Better than sex? Mike, when we get back to my house, we really need to try whatever they did last night."

"Malova, you are sick!"

"I know. I just can't help myself. It's a way of life."

"Naturally, it is for you. Anyways, let's talk shop about what I want for my wedding....."

The rest of the afternoon we talked about color schemes. Later, the guys left and we girls ended up hanging out and visiting the local bridal shops. I was truly having the time of my life.

The months went by fast and August was here. I had everything set: My dad was giving me away, all my friends were in my wedding, and my wedding dress was custom made by my grandmother. I went that route, as none of the shops we visited the day of the luncheon really stood out for me. October 15th was the day, and I was extremely nervous. So nervous in fact that I was shaking like a leaf. While getting dressed, Malova came into my room and started styling my hair.

"You are so lucky to have Wil. He's far better than any of your ex-boyfriends any day." she said.

"Yeah, I know. I just hope that the craziest one doesn't show up. In fact, I am sorry. Let's not mention him on my special day."

"I didn't mention him. You did, but that's beside the point. You are my best friend, and I love you. I share your happiness. And I hope that you'll never forget about our friendship, because I truly won't forget you."

"Why are you talking crazy? You act like I'm going away for good. It's just a honeymoon, and when I get back, you will know everything. You want to know why you'll know everything? Because you are my best friend, and you will always be. I love you, Malova."

We embraced warmly in each other's arms. As we were finishing up, my dad walked in.

"May I have a few words with my daughter?" said dad.
"Sure Mr. Taylor," said Malova. "No problem."

As Malova walked out, my dad came and stood behind me while I was looking at myself in the mirror. He had the biggest smile on his face. His expressed told the story of a proud father -- filled with joy and love.

"Your mother would be proud. I know I am," he said. My mom had been dead for fifteen years.
"I wish she was still here. I prayed last night, and I asked God to tell her that I'm happy. I hope in spirit she's at my wedding."
"She will be pumpkin. But for now, you keep Wil in check. If he in any way hurts you, I'd better be informed. Because no matter what age you may be, you are still my little girl, and I love you."
"I love you too; Dad and you don't have to worry about Wil. He's the real article here. I am lucky to have him."
"Luck has nothing to do with it, Dear. It's a blessing from God."
"That's true, dad, but I also want you to know that no matter what; you're still my number one guy."

I started crying, even though I had promised myself that I would not. This was the happiest day of my life, and nothing could change it. My father told me it was time, and I left the bedroom. The wedding was in our own home in the ballroom. Even though it's not quite what Wil wanted, it was more cost effective to have all the festivities here in the mansion. Even though Wil was pretty rich, he was very conservative of his spending.

The music was playing, and I was walking down the steps smiling. There was Wil standing between Malik and Gustavo. My girlfriends were standing on the other side of the men. All of the guests were family and friends that I was happy had come to share in my joy. Even though it seemed like a lifetime walking down the aisle, I was standing before the minister before I knew it.

"Who is giving this lovely bride away?" asked the minister.

"I, Vaughn Taylor, am giving my daughter away."

"Good, then let us proceed. We have come today to see William Masterton and Courtni Taylor be bonded in holy matrimony. Is there anyone today who objects?"

No one answered. Thank you Jesus!

"Good. Let us proceed. Do you, William Sloan Masterton, take Courtni Renee Taylor to be your lawfully wedded wife? To have and to hold, through sickness and in health, for richer or poorer; forsaking all others until death do you part?"

"I do, with all my heart." Wil replied.

"Do you, Courtni Renee Taylor, take William Sloan Masterton, to be your lawfully wedded husband, to have and to hold, through sickness and in health, for richer or poorer; forsaking all others until death do you part?"

"I do." I had a bowl full of tears in my eyes…tears of joy.

"As they exchange rings, the two have written their own love vows to each other. William, you may start."

"I never thought that this day would come. I always felt in my mind after we met that you would be the one. My heart told me to ask you. I take you, Courtni, to be my wedded wife. With deepest jubilation I receive you into my life that together we may be one. As is Christ to His body, the church, so I will be to you a loving and faithful husband. Always will I perform my headship over you, even as Christ does over me, knowing that His Lordship is one of the holiest desires for my life. I promise you my deepest love, my fullest devotion, my tender care. I promise to always put God first, and you second in my life. I vow that I will lead our lives into a life of faith and hope in Christ Jesus. Ever honoring God's guidance by His spirit through the Word, and so throughout life, no matter what may lie ahead of us, I pledge to you my life. That night on Valentine's Day, you made me the happiest man in the world. I promise you this day, and every day, that I will love you for all eternity."

As if I wasn't crying enough already; he had to make it worse. The man I love is standing before me, expressing his undying love. Who could have asked for anything more? I now, more than ever pray that I can be everything I need to be to this man...and more.

"I love you, Wil and I desire to be your wife. For years I have prayed that God would lead me to His choice, and I am confident that His will is being fulfilled today. Through the sufferings of my past, pressures of the present and the uncertainties of the future I promise to be faithful to you. I will love you, from this day forth. You can count on me to respect you as headship of our home. Christ told us that the wife must submit herself to her own husband as to the Lord. For as Christ is Head of His Church so is the husband head of his wife. I submit myself to you this day. For years I kept my faith in you and the love I knew was real between us. The first time I fell in love with you, was when you stood up for me in my house against a negative, opposing force from my past. That's when I realized how much I meant to you. You have always meant the world to me, and you always will, even beyond the grave."

Wil started to cry.

"I'm embarrassed." he said sobbing.

"Why?" I asked.

"I'm not one for tears, especially in front of a woman. Double especially on my wedding day with hundreds of people watching."

"It's okay to cry. Lord knows we'll share a valley of tears together. In addition, I'm happy that we will."

The whole crowd shared their "awe's". After everyone again grew quiet, the minister finished up the ceremony.

"Now by the power vested in me by the State of California and by the blessing of our Savior Jesus Christ. What God has joined together, let no man separate. It is my honor to announce you two as husband and wife. William, you may kiss your bride."

Wil grabbed me and landed a passionate kiss on my lips. Everyone in the crowd clapped and cheered. As soon as Wil and I were about to walk down the aisle together, the front doors of our home flung open. It was Anthony! I hadn't seen him since that day in my house and quite frankly, I could have gone without seeing him ever again. He was taller, and he had lots of facial hair. He kind oflooked like a wild beast. Anthony was still wanted for breaking out of jail. I couldn't believe he would risk coming here, knowing he could get caught.

"I didn't know you were the marrying type, rich boy." he said.

"What are you doing here?" said Wil.

"I came for the wedding, of course." replied Anthony.

"I didn't send you a wedding invitation, and there was a reason."

"Courtni, I see Wil has you well trained already. You're lucky. I couldn't tame her for the world."

"Get out!" shouted Wil.

"Not before I kiss the bride."

Anthony grabbed me, and made an attempt to kiss me. I punched him in the jaw, and as he started falling to the ground, I hiked up the front part of my wedding dress and kicked him in the groin. He tripped me, and grabbed the back of my hair.

"Let me go! You're hurting me." I shouted.

"I haven't begun to hurt you yet. I'm going to repay you in full for all that you have done to me. Payback starts now and trust me; I'm signing all the checks."

Malik and Gustavo started kicking him in the face. Greg helped me up and dusted my dress off. The boys, as well as my father-in-law Sloan, carried him out the front door.

"If you ever come near my son or my daughter in law, I'll kill you. You are just as reckless as your father! Malik and Gustavo will tend to your needs some more." said Sloan.

They carried Anthony to the back alley and continued to beat him. All anyone could hear was a bunch of ouches and bashing in the alley. Once they were done with him, they came back into the house to wash their hands. Wil ran over and held me close to him.

"Baby, are you hurt?" Wil asked.

"No, I'm just angry beyond comprehension right now."

"Are you up for a reception?

"Of course I am. Like I said before, I'm not going to let anything or anyone ruin this day for me."

Even though I was satisfied with the beating Malik and Gustavo gave Anthony, Varsha still recommended that I call the police. By the time they got there, Anthony was long gone.

The police said there was a trail of blood that leads into the street. I came to the conclusion that even though he was badly beaten, he was still able to get on his motorcycle and ride off. I wanted him behind bars…hell I wanted him out of my life, but it looked like that wasn't going to happen any time soon.

My reception was everything I hoped. I had no worries at all, except one: Is Anthony going to live up to his promise?

Chapter Eight

Wil and I were on one of his company's private jets. I had changed my clothes on the plane, since I wasn't sure where we were going. I hope it's somewhere exciting! While he was reading a magazine, I was looking out the window smiling. I can't believe that I'm married. I must be the luckiest girl in the world to have a wonderful, loving (don't forget rich) husband.

"Wil, where are we going?"

"If I tell you, it won't be a surprise." he replied.

"You always have to be difficult, don't you?"

"I'm not trying to be difficult my love….I just don't want to ruin the surprise. Anyway, are you happy my darling?"

"Yes, but I am worried about something."

"What's that?"

"The person who crashed our wedding is what. He looked like he was serious. I know he's gonna' try to hurt us somehow. I just feel it."

"Anthony Merrick is a pompous pig. He's all talk and the action that he displays is ignorance. All he is trying to do is scare you into submitting to his will. I know that you have faith; I can see it shining through you, but it's very dim. I am going to pray for you to have strength and trust in your faith in God that He will handle this. The Lord already has this situation under control."

"You're right, honey. I just get so frustrated with….."

"Faith; remember?"

"Okay, I am going to work on it."

"And besides, I need you to pray for me as well because if he ever touches you, I will kill him. You would have to come visit me in jail and pray the Lord has mercy on my soul!"

"That is the last thing I want."

"Look, I have ties with the police department. If it would make you feel better, I'll call Chief Martin and file for a restraining order against him. Would that be okay with you?"

"Sure. That would help me feel a little better about the situation."

When the plane landed, I noticed that we were in a beautiful city. I've never traveled outside of California, but I knew we weren't in that state. It was dark outside but the city lights gave off a radiant accent of the city skyline. As I was exiting from the plane, I grabbed my bags. My husband stood at the steps, held my hand to help me off the plane, and we stood in the airfield waiting for a limo.

"Wil, what is this place?"

"I remembered one of our conversations stating that you had never been outside of California, and if you had your chance to leave, you'd visit one place."

"Wil, you didn't..."

We saw the limousine coming behind us. The driver came to a slow roll, lowered his window and said, "Welcome to New Orleans, Mr. and Mrs. Masterton!"

I was surprised and grateful at the same time. "Thank you, Wil! This is a wonderful and pleasant surprise."

He embraced me in his arms and replied, "You are most welcome; anything for my wife. This is just a taste to prove that if I can do or be it for you; I am ready, willing and able. So, what do you want to do first?"

"Shopping of course!"

We toured almost everywhere in New Orleans: The Bayou, Bourbon Street, restaurants, shopping plazas, etc. After giving my credit cards a workout, we checked in at the

St. Christopher Hotel in the French Quarter. It was beautiful with a southern charm, warm with that "at home" feeling.

It was about nine o'clock when we got up to our room. Wil picked me up and carried me over the threshold. The room was gorgeous. It looked like an apartment without a kitchen. Wil placed me on the couch, and we started watching movies together. I started to get a little hungry, so I ordered Game Birds Mediterranean Style from the dining room. When the bell hop arrived with my food, we decided to share the food together in front of the well lit fireplace.

"This is great!"
"Yes it is." he replied.
"I hope the rest of our life is as enjoyable as this."
"Don't worry. It will be."
"The fire is dying off. I think I saw the wood cupboard by the bedroom. I'll go and get some more." I got up, but he pulled me back down to the floor.
"There's no need for it. Besides, I can be your fire."
"Oh really?"
"Indeed," he came closer to me. He wrapped his arms around me tight. This was the moment I had been waiting for, and I couldn't help but shiver. My body was trembling and he felt it. Wil started caressing my shoulders and said, "You don't have to be nervous. I'll be gentle while I make love to you. All you have to do is relax and let go."

With that he gave me the most passionate kiss. I was so happy and anxious. I could feel myself rising with a craving, a lust for him to be inside me. By the look in his eyes, I could tell he wanted me just as much as I wanted him. Wil slowly took off my clothes, piece by piece, until virtually every article was on the floor at my feet. He lifted me, and carried me into the bedroom. When we got there, Wil placed me on the bed, and he started running his tongue down my neck while slowly taking off my bra and garter. The heat and lust were rising inside of me. I couldn't take it anymore; I wanted him so badly that I felt like crying. I ripped off all of his clothes, and forced him inside me. He was so hard and soothing. My imagination had nothing on the actual feeling of it. He held my hands above my head and stared at me with his sexy, piercing eyes. "Be patient," he says, "We have all the time in the world for that." He slowly withdrew himself from my body and got on his knees kissing my thighs gently; slowly coming up in between my legs with his tongue licking me gently. I was moaning and shaking. It felt better than the first time he pleased me this way. My moans became louder and louder until they turned into screams. I grabbed his head holding it in place for my orgasm. My body became tense and then I let out a loud, lustful yell. After my body relaxed, he came up to the lips on my face and kissed me. I could taste myself on his tongue, which turned me on even more. He rolled over on the bed lying on his back, and placed me on top of him. I positioned myself to where he could gently slip himself inside of me. It was slow and sexy at first until I decided to pick up the pace. Even then I was cumming all over him. As I went faster and harder, he moaned louder and louder. He picked me up again and placed me on my back. Wil whispered, "This was well worth the wait." While sliding inside of me slowly, he whispered in my ear, "I love you so much, Courtni." With every forward thrust, I could feel him getting harder. I felt so weak but it was a comfortable state to be in. I was trying my best not to moan so much, but I was powerless. He was kissing me softly on my neck as he went faster, he continued to whisper in my ear, "I can't believe I waited until this long. You feel so good." With that, Wil grabbed the back of my hair and gently pulled it. As I was starting to cum again, I felt him releasing inside me. He pulled my hair tighter and raised his head to look at me. With sweat dripping from his forehead, down to my cheek, he looked at me and told me he loved me again. I pulled him closer and gave him a hard, passionate kiss and told him I loved him back. I tried to inch away. Wil pulled my hair and lowered my head back to the bed. "Oh, I'm not done yet, Mrs. Masterton. I'm just getting started." He wasn't kidding. We made love in the same fashion repeatedly; all through the night.

The rest of our honeymoon was fabulous. We did more shopping, hung out in the French Quarter and checked out the St. Charles Street Car. Let's not forget the incredible sex we had every night the entire time we were there.

Once we got back home, everything was lovely. We turned my old bedroom into my studio. Clients were coming in like crazy; especially once they found out I was married to Wil. His businesses were booming as well. He tripled his revenue over three month's time.

Though everything was going smoothly on our individual fronts, our marriage was starting to get shaky. We didn't fight, but Wil was extremely busy. There was a certain person who was trying to take over his company. He spent most of his time at the office and would tell me small details, but nothing much to go on. He would call everyday to express his vows of love, but it wasn't the same as seeing him at home before ten o'clock at night. I was also going through some changes on my own. After I would help Margarette, our maid, clean the house, I would eat and sleep. I didn't even have the energy to go shopping. One day, Malova came over to see me.

"We were supposed to have dinner when you came back….that was three months ago," she started, "Where have you been?"
"At home."
"At home! Girl, you better get your ass up. It's a beautiful day outside."
"I know, but I haven't been feeling right lately."
"You do look a little pale. Are you alright?"
"I don't know. I was reading this parenting book, and I have some of the symptoms of being pregnant."

"Pregnant? Damn, that must have been some honeymoon."

"It was. He took me to New Orleans; we shopped, ate, made love, and slept."

"I see. Therefore, the sex must have it going on."

"Oh my, going on doesn't even adequately describe the experience. He's the best I have ever had. "

"You go, girl. Hey, I'll call Dr. Carbords and have him to check you out."

"You don't have to do that. I have a home pregnancy test in the bathroom cabinet. I just haven't built up the guts to use it."

"If you want me to stay with you while you take it, I'll be glad to."

"Thanks. That really means a lot."

I cleaned myself up, and I took the test. The instructions stated that results show up in five minutes. Those five minutes felt like an eternity. At last it was time. I was too nervous to look. Malova went in the bathroom for me.

"So?"

"Do you want to be pregnant?" she asked.

"I don't know. We really haven't discussed kids in depth. Lately, he hasn't even been around enough for us to discuss anything. Why? What did it say?"

"Well, can I be the godmother?"

"I'm really pregnant?"

"Yes ma'am. The line is a solid, bright blue line. Now, all you have to do is call the doctor to determine how far along you are. How did you get pregnant that quick?"

"Well I guess all the sex on the honeymoon did it."

"When are you gonna' tell him?"

"He's been so busy. I don't know."

"You better tell him soon. I think he would be a little mad if he had to figure it out on his own."

"Tell me about it. Can you believe that we've had our very first "fight"?"

"Really? What happened?"

"While on our honeymoon, there was this maid trying to holla' at Wil; I knew that she liked him because when we first got to New Orleans, she was in the lobby. Her eyes were fixed on Wil. I didn't say anything at first. Then she started coming up to our room a lot. I still didn't say anything. One day, I had just come back from shopping. The door was cracked and I heard her talking dirty to my husband."

"What was she saying?"

"Your wife doesn't really know what she's got. I bet she doesn't know how to suck it correctly. I got some time....I could show you. I was truly pissed. I stormed in that room, grabbed her by her hair, and threw her out of our room like a Frisbee."

"Girl, you are off the chain! I still don't understand why you and Wil fought."

"He said that was totally uncalled for."

"Totally uncalled for my ASS! Let me hear a bitch try to talk to Mike like that, and she knows I could be around. Oh wee...."

"That's what I said. He fussed at me for awhile. He said he loved only me, and if he wanted some eighteen year old slut, he'd teach high school. I thought about it and apologized. We were both laughing at that Frisbee toss though. And to top it all off, we went back to the bedroom and made love."

"Not trying to take sides, but he does have a point. He married you, Courtni and you have to admit, he's fine. You are going to have to deal with women trying to scope your man out for the rest of your lives. You are so lucky, though. I wish I could get Mike on all fours and ask me to marry him....oh shit, look at the time. I got to meet Mike for dinner. I'll call you."

Malova kissed me on the cheek and ran out the door. I laid on the couch thinking about my recent news. I'm going to be a mother; it's something that I am excited about, but completely unprepared for. The phone was ringing, so I had to go answer it.

"Hello." I said.

"Hey honey! How are you?" said Wil.

"I'm cool. I'm just sitting on the couch, eating crackers, and just chillin'."

"Are you dressed?"

"Yeah a little bit, why?"

"There is this hearing I have to attend, and I want you to be there with me."

"Sure honey, but why do I have to go to it?"

"Well, you really don't have to, but I would prefer that you be there with me. I believe you may be able to shed some light on some things. I found out who was trying to take over my business. It's Anthony."

"Anthony! How can he be suing you? He's wanted for murder and breaking out of jail! How can he run businesses? He didn't even finish high school."

"Some of the best business people I know don't have a high school diploma. I found out through my dad that Anthony's father used to work for him a long time ago. To cut to the chase in this matter, in my dad's business contract clause, no one can be owner or part owner of any of his businesses if you have a criminal background…"

"Oh, well he definitely has that. He has outstanding warrants!"

"Well from what I've been told, he paid off the judge to drop all charges against him."

"Okay, but what about Anthony breaking out of jail?"

"He's on probation for that."

"I can't believe this! He continues to get away with murder, literally! Sure he's been busted for plenty other stuff, but it's nothing in comparison to what he was in jail for."

"Every dog has their day, Courtni. God has this all worked out…even though we can't see it."

"I know honey, but it's frustrating…"

"He's says be still and know that I am the Lord…."

"Alright. I get the picture!"

"I more or less want you there for moral support, but if you don't want to come, I completely understand."

"Of course I'll come, sweetheart; I'm already dressed because Malova came over. Do you want me to meet you at the courthouse or do you want to pick me up?"

"If you can meet me there, it would be great."

"That's fine. In fact, I'll call Malova. Her testimony can also be relevant because her brother and Anthony got most of their criminal records together."

"Great! I'll see you shortly."

Anthony Merrick? Business conscious? No way! I called Malova, and told her to meet us at the courthouse. Mike wasn't too happy about it because she was cooking him dinner. At 7:30, everyone was assembled together. My father in law flew in from Memphis, and he didn't look very happy at all, but could anyone blame him? Anthony walked in late, but that was certainly not a surprise.

"Where there's one, there's the other." said Anthony.

"I still can't believe you got off on all charges."

"Believe it, baby. I'm the man, but you already knew that."

"I'm not your baby, and besides, don't you have something else better to do?"

"Of course I do….like taking over your husband's legacy and his life. Maybe I'll have enough money to win you back."

"In your dreams, Merrick!"

Sam Gales was the judge proceeding over the case. I knew of him from reading the papers on other cases he handled. He had a reputation for being a real hard ass and no one has ever been able to buy his ruling. In our case, I thought it would be a fair trial. After he reached his bench, he told us to be seated. Wil, Sloan, Malova, and I was on one side; Anthony and his attorney, Shacobian Myers, were on the other. Shacobian was California's most successful business law attorney. Rumor has it that he has never lost a case. Seeing him had me kind of worried about the situation.

"Now," started the judge, "it says here that Anthony Jacob Merrick is entitled to Masterton Incorporated because your father, Boris Merrick was Sloan Masterton's partner. Is this correct?"

"Yes, your honor." replied Anthony.

"Well, all the proper papers seem to be here. Now, I would like to hear from you Sloan why you and your son will not share."

"Your honor," said Wil," I wouldn't mind sharing with Mr. Merrick, but there are some factors that should be looked at."

"I asked for Sloan to speak, but I will accept statements from you, William....explain."

"Thank you, your honor. Anthony Merrick has a laundry list of felonies. Per the clause in the contract between my father and Boris Merrick, the contract is void if either party has a criminal record. Also, Anthony Merrick has terrorized my wife and me for years. So much, in fact, that we do have a restraining order that has been filed and is currently being enforced. My wife frequently visits all of the businesses, and if she and Mr. Merrick happen to be in one of them together, he would be in violation of the restraining order."

"Do you have a copy of the contract clause and the restraining order?"

"Yes, your honor. If you will allow me to approach the bench I can give you the documentation."

"Bring it up," Wil walked to the judge's platform and gave him several papers. He looked them over with a puzzled look on this face. He placed the papers in a folder. "Looks like things are in order; this is a valid restraining order. However, this is not enough for me to say that he is not entitled to his half of the companies."

"You are correct, your honor." said Shacobian, "I am well aware that my client has a restraining order against him for Courtni Masterton. Masterton Incorporated is made up of ten different businesses. Both parties can have five businesses each and since the order is in place against my client, Mrs. Masterton can avoid the businesses that Mr. Merrick owns."

"Thank you, Mr. Myers, but according to this other document that has been placed before me, Mr. Merrick does have a list of felonies and misdemeanors. How can your client substantiate his right to half of the businesses with this clause in affect?"

"If you will review this document," Mr. Myers approached the bench and handed the judge a different document. "This proves that all charges that were brought up against my client have been dropped. With regards to him allegedly breaking out of jail, he chose to take probation for that offense instead of wasting tax payer's money on another trial. My client has done a service to the community by taking that route." The alleged breaking out of jail? What the....how can you....okay this guy was really pissing me off. Nevertheless, I guess you get what you pay for, and I have to give Anthony props for paying a lot of money to a damn good lawyer.

"Well put, Mr. Myers, though I don't completely buy what you're saying. Are there any other records that will prove useful to state your claim against Mr. Merrick?" asked the judge.

"Actually your honor," Malova stood up, "I may have some evidence to bring to that table."

"And you are?"

"Malova Annette Brown. I have proof that Mr. Merrick would be in violation of the contract due to his criminal background."

"Miss Brown, we have just addressed this part...."

"But there's something that Shacobian Myers didn't catch in his research."

"Alright, please state your case."

"Your honor, I am a compliance clerk for the FDA, and I was able to pull records of a complaint filed against Mr. Merrick and his father. Boris Merrick almost caused La Bonita to lose their license due to suspicions of Argo-terrorism. In 1999, there were reports of fruit containing an extremely addictive, yet harmful virus. The organism that causes the virus was a man-made organism, and Anthony Merrick was tied to a chemist by the name of Barry Xavier, who was the creator of the organic virus. One of the charges that Mr. Merrick had brought upon him was Argo-terrorism. As you can see for yourself, your honor, the proper documentation is right here, and it is still an open case, it has not been dropped."

The judge studied the FDA documents. I noticed the look on Anthony's face. He started squirming in his seat and a scowl came across his face. Anthony knew he was busted.

"Also, your honor," Malova continued, "I know Mr. Merrick on a personal level. My brother Daidus Brown and Mr. Merrick have had plenty of run-ins with the law in their youth as well as recently. They both were arrested for drug trafficking back in 1995. I have the arrest papers right here; also another case not dropped."

"Thank you, Miss Brown. Now, Mr. Myers, did you have any record of your client's action as related to the FDA case?" asked the judge.

"No your honor," Shacobian answered, "I was not aware of these allegations."

"They are more than allegations. I expected more from you, Mr. Myers. The next time you take on a case, you need to do your normal profiling on your clients, because you have now just experienced your first loss in court. It is the decision of this court that Anthony Merrick has no claim to Masterton

Incorporated due to the violation on file with the FDA, as well as proof of breach of contract by having criminal activity on file. Case dismissed!"

Everyone started walking outside. As I approached the door, Anthony pulled me towards him.

"You little bitch! This is your fault!" he shouted. He had an angry look on his face. "If you would have kept your mouth shut......"

"Look here," I was outraged and definitely pissed off,

"Not that I owe you an explanation, but if you noticed, I didn't speak during the entire hearing."

"You gave them information about the restraining order."

"That wasn't even the reason why you lost!"

"Then you brought Malova here. If her brother knew she was selling us out behind his back..."

"I am sick and tired of you and your lame excuses for why you fail! This could have been avoided if you hadn't called yourself trying to ruin people's lives. You are nothing but a worthless bum. You have messed with me for the last time. If you say one more thing to me, so help me –"Wil came over and grabbed me.

"Honey, I'll handle –"

"Let go of me, William!"

"Yes ma'am." He threw his hands in the air and backed away from Anthony and me.

"What are you gonna do to me, Courtni? You've always been too scared to stand up to me. You're nothing!"

That was the last straw, and I finally could do something I should have done years ago. I landed a well placed punch to Anthony's face. He fell to the ground, and even before he hit the ground, my fists kept a steady flow of hits to his face. Malova came over to me and tried to pull me off. Rage fueled my adrenaline and I continued beating the shit out of him.

"Wil, help me! She's out of control!" shouted Malova.

They grabbed my arms, but then I started kicking him. When I landed a blow to his stomach, everything became dim until I was overcome with the darkness.

I woke up to see Wil hovering over me. I must have been out for a while, because we were in our bedroom.

"What happened?" I asked.
"When Malova and I were trying to get you off of Anthony, you collapsed. Malova told me that you were in no condition to be fighting. What did she mean?"
"Wil, I didn't want to tell you this until after the trial was over. Remember when you said you wanted to start a family?"
"Yeah."
"Well, we're going to be starting one sooner than I thought. I'm pregnant, William."

Chapter Nine

"Pregnant?" asked Wil.

"Yeah, you aren't mad, are you?"

"Are you kidding me? You just made me the happiest man in Long Beach."

He held me tightly in his arms. I smiled with relief.

"Is there anything I can get you?" he asked.

"I could go for some grape juice." I replied.

"Margarette! Get some grape juice! Why did you charge after Anthony if you knew you were pregnant?"

"Baby, I'm sorry. He made me so mad. I could have killed him."

"You looked as if you were going to. Well, that's behind you. How many months are you?"

"I am not sure, but I speculate that I am about three months."

"Three? Oh my! I have to call doctors, nurses, set up ultra sounds, and...."

"Honey, take it one day at a time."

"Okay. You better not get into anymore fights. Do you understand me?"

"Yes sir."

"Good. Now, is there anything else I can get you?"

"In fact there is," I came close up to him. I was kissing behind his ear. "You can get undressed and make love to me right now."

"Honey, do you think it's safe in your condition?"

"Don't worry about my condition," I started kissing on his neck. I massaged my hands all over his body. His eyes were rolling in the back of his head. "Just worry about yours."

"You know, you are becoming very persistent. I think it's sexy."

"I always have been."

I walked over to the CD player, and put in one of my favorite mixed CDs. The sound of "If Tomorrow Never Comes" filled my ears and my soul. I started swaying my hips to the rhythm while walking over to Wil. I danced myself into his arms, and beckoned him to join me with my seducing eyes. We undressed each other slowly, and a gently pushed him on the bed. I toppled on top of him. My hips were perfectly positioned to take his stiff erection inside of me. I rode him to the rhythm of the song that was playing – riding him until we both erupted with passion.

Month after month, I noticed the changes in my mind, body and moods. Wil and I decided to wait to see what we were having. I always liked the old fashioned way; it makes the experience more exciting. We hadn't heard from Anthony again, which was a blessing, but I couldn't help wondering how long it would stay that way. I prayed that I would never see or hear from him again. However, in the depths of my heart and soul, I just knew I hadn't heard the last of him.

I was six months into my pregnancy, and I felt as big as a house. I would attempt to help Margarette clean, but Wil always fussed at me to go and sit down. I would get so tired -- no matter what it was I was trying to do. In my mind, I had turned into a worthless wife. One day, Malova and Varsha came over.

"Oh! Getting a little large, aren't we?" Varsha asked.
"Shut up!"
"Six months of pregnancy, and you haven't lost your mind yet?" asked Malova. "I'm proud of you."
"Who says I haven't lost it? I could just be well composed right now."
"Are you up for a wedding?" asked Varsha.
"Not really, but which one of you is getting married?" I asked with excitement. I sat up on the couch. I was thinking to myself, It's Varsha and Greg.

"We both are!" they shouted.

"A double wedding? That's great! I knew Varsha and Greg would eventually, but you and Mike? I'm shocked."

"It took him long enough. I thought he would never ask." said Malova.

"Well, we are talking about the same man that spent years in denial and then was just scared to say something."

"This is true. In fact, I've been holding out on you. The day of Anthony's trial was the day he proposed. Well, he proposed after I got back home. That's why he was mad that I had to leave."

"I am so sorry, Malova."

"Don't be. He said it gave him enough time to really contemplate if this is what he really wanted, and if he not only could go through with this, but also if he was truly ready to spend the rest of his life with me. When I walked in the door, he was on both knees with the ring box; he was in tears begging me to marry him. Of course I couldn't say no -- especially since I would have married him at least two years ago if he had asked."

"I am happy for all four of you. Where's my invitation?"

"Girl," said Varsha, "now you know you're our matron of honor."

"I am?"

"Of course! We couldn't have a wedding without you." said Malova.

"But I don't know. Wil's been ragging on me a lot these days. He's always shouting, *rest and relax*. He might not let me be in this wedding. Can you all wait until after I have the baby?"

"I think we've waited long enough and besides all you'll be doing is walking down the aisle." said Varsha.

"And Anthony won't be there," says Malova, "I made sure of that."

"Okay, I'll do it."

We spent the rest of our time laughing and talking. It seemed as if everything and everyone in my life was balanced again. Around 8:00P.M., Wil was home. I wanted to soften him up, so I made an amazing steak dinner. He was a little aggravated because he felt I was on my feet to long, but he was grateful. During the dessert, I decided to tell him about the wedding.

"Honey," I started, "you won't believe whose getting married."

"Who?"

"Varsha, Greg, Malova, and Mike. It's going tobe a double wedding."

"That's great. When?"

"In a month."

"Good. We'll have time to get them a wedding present."

"Sweetheart, they've asked me to be their matron of honor."

"Courtni, you know that the doctor said you shouldn't be too active and..."

"All I'm going to do is walk down the aisle, taking pictures, and slow dancing with you."

"That's active. Furthermore, I know they didn't ask for you to the photographer too."

"No. Don't be silly. I'm going to have one of my photo apprentices to take the professional photos."

"I don't think it's a good idea for you to do so much."

"Wil please let me do this. They were in our wedding. I want to return the favor."

"But neither you nor they were pregnant with doctor's orders when we got married."

"Please?"

"Will Anthony be there?"

"No. Malova said she made sure that he wouldn't be there. I don't know how she arranged that, but I trust her at her word."

"That actually puts a nice spin on it. I don't need him complicating anything else in our lives. Alright, but I want you to be careful. No dress with a long train and any high heeled shoes are out."

"Thank you. I love you."

"I love you, too."

Preparing for their wedding was much more fun than mine. Both Malova and Varsha were very picky about their dresses and the church. They even were stressing out over the tuxes because the boys wanted different things. It took a couple of months, but they got everything together. Before we knew it, March was upon us, and I was eight months pregnant. It was a beautiful day; my friends were getting married. The wedding was taking place at All Saints Evangelical Free Church. On the day of the wedding, I was in the dressing room trying to get ready. Malova handed me my dress, which was cute, but would have been cuter if I weren't pregnant. After she left the room, I started crying uncontrollably. I must have been really loud because Wil came in order to check on me.

"Courtni, what's wrong?" he asked.

"I'm fat and ugly! I look like a beached whale!"

"No, you don't. Baby, you're pregnant. You're supposed to be big."

"Not helping, William! You're depressing me more."

"Oh honey, I'm sorry. I still love you. In fact, I love you more than I ever did before. "

"Then why you never want to make love anymore?"

"Sweetheart now is not the time to address this issue."

"I think it is. You have not touched me since the night I made your steak dinner. Just be honest with me and tell me you don't find me attractive while I'm pregnant!"

"Courtni, I do find you attractive -- no matter what. The reason why we haven't made love is because the doctor said that it isn't healthy for the baby -- especially now that you are this far along. Considering the earlier complications, due to stress and anxiety, being intimate this far along could be dangerous."

"He never told me."

"That's because he didn't want to depress you. However, you look great in that dress."

"Whatever! I'd better go check on Varsha and Malova now."

"Okay, but I meant what I said."

He gave me a quick kiss, and he was off. I went to the green room to check on the girls. They looked both stunning and nervous. Both were pacing back and forth.

"Hey, what's wrong?"

"We're nervous." said Malova.

"I can see that."

"What if something goes wrong?"

"What if Anthony shows up? I don't want him to ruin my wedding too." added Varsha.

"I thought that was taken care of?" I replied.

"That's only for the wedding, but the reception is a different story."

"Are you kidding me? Well, I refuse to let that joker keep me down. This is supposed to be the happiest day of your lives. The men you love are finally showing their vows of love. Moreover, I'm rejoicing that I'm here to see it. You both are the only true friends I've had. I'm not going to let anyone ruin this for you. I love you guys too much to let that happen."

"Wait one minute," said Malova, "I thought I was the strong one. You're outshining me."

"Somebody has got to be strong right now. It might as well be me."

"Thanks Courtni. It means a lot." said Varsha.

"It means a lot to us both." replied Malova.

The wedding ceremony was beautiful, except the part where I walked down the aisle looking like the Goodyear blimp. It didn't matter though, because I had never seen my friends happier. They chose to have their reception at La Bonita. Besides the gift cards, we purchased for all of them, it was also a part of Wil, and I's wedding gift to them. The music was jamming. Wil wouldn't let me dance due to the pregnancy. During the middle of the evening, I convinced Wil that there wasn't any harm in one slow dance, so we started dancing next to Varsha and Greg. Mike and Malova had to leave early on account of their flight to Spain. There was a loud roar of a motorcycle engine outside. The doors burst open, and it was Anthony. His appearance was the same as our last meeting, only his beard was a little longer.

"Sorry I'm late," he was saying, "but we all know how traffic can be."

"Get out of here, Anthony." said Greg.

"What is your problem? Why do you always show up to events that you aren't even invited to?" said Wil.

"You have nothing to say to me. You took something away from me that was partially mine." said Anthony.

"I didn't take anything from you. In fact, why am I even having this conversation with you? You need to leave!"

"This is a public place, and you cannot make me leave unless I start to cause trouble. I haven't started any…yet."

"This is a public place owned by me and at this time a private event is being held. La Bonita is not open to the public this evening, as denoted on the sign outside. Besides, you being here is also a violation of your restraining order."

"Anthony, go home." I wasn't in the mood for anyone's attitude. Even though this was a happy event, I was tired; and the fact that I was feeling hot and corpulent made it clear that I was not about to take any unnecessary crap from anyone -- especially him.

"Courtni, you've gotten bigger. Pregnant are we?" Anthony asked.

"You are disturbing our peace -- especially mine. Get out before you get your ass kicked again!" Lord, forgive me, but he is really pissing me off!

"I have a permanent reminder of my embarrassment, thank you. Since we are on the subject of that, you went completely overboard. I didn't know you could throw a punch. Hell, if I wasn't so damn impressed by it, I would have pressed charges!"

"You are a sick-minded individual, do you know that? Impressed? Why? I would have been embarrassed knowing that I got my ass kicked by my pregnant ex-girlfriend!"

"Well, isn't that special? You still have that damn mouth on you with balls attached. Doesn't matter because you are still going to pay, Courtni, for what you did to me. You and your husband ruined my life."

"Your life was already ruined. We had nothing to do with that. Start taking accountability for your own actions and stop blaming everyone else!"

"You know, I'm sick and tired of your mouth. You need to fix it. It's obvious that Wil doesn't know how to tame a woman."

"First of all, no one can tame me. You couldn't even get a hold of me like you wanted to. That's one of the many reasons you cheated on me. Second, with regards to shutting me up, what are you gonna do? Come and shut me up?"

"If you force me to, I will."

"Save your menaces for someone who is frightened by them. You should know by now that I will take you any day of the week!"

Anthony came toward me. He looked unbalanced, but he didn't scare me. Wil stepped in front of me.

"I swear, if you touch her..." said Wil.

"Move, Wil!"

"Courtni, I won't let you argue with him. Let alone fight him."

"Did you not hear me say move?" Wil stood his ground and refused to move out of the way. I was mad as hell, but at the same time I understood why, and I respected him for being a man willing to stand up for his family. Anthony and Wil were face to face. It was like a show down at The Apollo.

"You've got a lot of balls to face me off like this. Last time your wife put you in your place, and you got out of the way." replied Anthony.

"Jesus, have mercy on my soul for the actions and words I am about to display, but I am tired of your shit, man! With regards to having balls, I've always had them; but I usually allow the Lord to fight my battles."

"So what's different today?"

"Today is the day I take matters into my own hands. I'm going to knock your punk ass out, and then you're getting the hell out of here, and out of our lives!"

"You're gonna be sorry. I swear to that."

"Anthony, I've realized something," I started, "you think you're cool because you have your good looks, your drug money and your so-called smooth lines. Well, beauty is only skin deep, and you're an ugly person. At my wedding, I was so scared that you were gonna live out your threat."

"I still am."

"It doesn't scare me. You don't scare me. When I met Wil, I finally got my life back."

"You're nothing without me."

"No! You're nothing without me! I made you into a prince, but now you're upset because I took your crown. You ain't shit, Anthony. As far as me, well I'm everything you desired to be, and you can't do anything to take that away from me."

"Furthermore, asshole, Courtni is everything without you. She has become much more than she was before. She has ascended to a higher level. You could never have been that for her because you are too much in love with the devil and yourself." said Wil.

"How dare either of you! Courtni, you were a little girl who was stupid and careless..."

"Yeah, I was a little girl. Now, I'm a woman who doesn't need a Ken doll to have fun."

"Keep talkin'. I'll slap you!"

"You will try to slap her, but you have to get through me and that is impossible." said Wil.

"Once again, with the threats! Listen here, you don't run me anymore. I'm wearing the dress, suit, boxing glove, the big balls, and I'm gonna' wear your ass out. I dare you to raise your hand to me. And William, if you try to stop me, I'll kick your ass too."

Wil stepped to the side, but he was still in arms length of Anthony and me. Anthony made an attempt to slap me, but I grabbed his hand. I heard a snap in his wrist, and I threw him over the dinner table. Just as Anthony was about to charge at me again, the police rushed in. "Hold it right there, Anthony!" The detective came in the side door.

"Mr. Merrick," the detective started, "we have a warrant for your arrest."

"A warrant? For what?" Anthony shouted.

"Remember the judge you paid off to have the murder charges dropped against you at that nightclub incident? Well looks like he had a change of heart. You are under arrest for the murders at The Whiz night club, arson, breaking out of jail and damage to a state penitentiary. And let's not forget, you are currently in violation of your restraining order that was put in place by Mrs. Masterton."

"I want to press charges for assault! She broke my wrist!"

"From what we could tell it was self defense, so pressing charges against her isn't valid. We have an ambulance outside. I'll have him look at it for you. Detectives Malik and Gustavo will escort you to the ambulance."

With smiles on their faces, good ole' Malik and Gustavo grabbed Anthony. They roughed him up and put him in handcuffs. As they were taking him away, he extended his leg and tripped me.

"I'm gonna get you, Courtni. I'm gonna find you, and I'm gonna kill you."

"I am so worried. Wil, come and help me up." I said. I was feeling pretty good. Finally got the satisfaction of telling Anthony how I really felt. I never knew I could be so pernicious, and yet have some much peace.

"Courtni Renee' Masterton, don't you ever do that again. You could have gotten hurt." he chastised.

"But I didn't so there's nothing to worry about. Well.... oh shit..." I felt a warm, wet sensation running down my leg. Disgusting! "Wil, I think my water broke."

"Your water broke! Oh my God! Greg, go outside and see if that ambulance has left yet. Courtni's going to have the baby."

The longer I stood there, the more pressure I felt on my uterus, almost like my baby was trying to find its way out. My heart was fluttering because I was so nervous. Was I about to lose my baby?

The ambulance kicked Anthony out and got me on the stretcher with urgency. I was rushed to Acts Hospital. Dr. Carbords came to the ambulance. He, his assistants, and Wil carried me out of the ambulance. The pains in my lower abdomen were increasing. I started screaming in agony. It felt like something was trying to rip out of my body. I let out another scream and then the room grew dark.

When I woke up, I was in the Women and Infants unit of the hospital. The doctor came in with a mask and gloves on.

"Mrs. Masterton, I'm Dr. Sanders. I'm assisting Dr. Carbords since you are about to have a premature baby. We ran some tests, and we see nothing wrong. Your baby is going to be perfectly healthy; a little small, but healthy."

"That's a relief. Where is my husband?"

"He's with the registration nurse admitting you. He'll be with you shortly."

"When can I start pushing?" The pain was growing stronger.

"Are you in pain, Mrs. Masterton?"

"What kind of doctor are you? Don't you deliver babies all the time? Of course I am in pain. Can I get something to ease it?"

"You are too far along to give you an epidural. You are at 7 ½ centimeters. As soon as your husband comes, you can start to push."

"Do we have to wait on him?"

"If you dilate any more, then we won't be able to. Besides, don't you want him to experience the wonders of child birth with you?"

"Yes, but if he doesn't hurry up, I'm starting without him."

Wil rushed in wearing his scrubs, mask, and gloves. Dr. Carbords followed behind him.

"Darling," he said out of breath, "are you ready to start pushing?"

"I've been ready."

"Alright then. Let's begin." Dr. Sanders said.

As I was pushing, the pain was more than I could bear. It felt like I was constipated five times over -- on top of the world's worst menstrual cramps!

"Push!" shouted Dr Carbords.

"I am pushing." I replied.

"Honey, you're going to have to push harder." said Wil.

"Oh you shut up! You're the reason why I'm in this."

"No, you're the reason why you're in this. If you wouldn't have been Miss Billy Bad Ass, you would be at home right now."

"Don't blame me for this...aaaah! Get it out! Now!"

I heard a little baby cry.

"Mrs. Masterton, you have a little baby girl." replied Dr. Sanders. I started crying, but I wasn't sure if it was because it was a girl or the fact that I was happy the pain was over. I'd have to say it was a bit of both. The nurse placed her in my arms. She was beautiful. Her eyes, nose, and lips were tiny. She looked up at me and smiled. Wil stood next to me.

"We did it, sweetheart." said Wil.

"Yeah, we did."

"She is truly precious; she sort of looks like me."

"She has your captivating eyes, Wil."

"She has your wonderful smile and your button nose."

"You're real cute, Wil."

"Sorry! I didn't mean anything by it. And besides, I like your nose."

"It's too late to suck up now."

"So, what do you want to name her?"

"If you don't mind, I want to name her after my mother, Ricci Cassandra. I promised my mother if I ever had kids, that I would name my first girl after her."

"That's no problem. Ricci Cassandra Masterton it is."

The nurse came back and placed Ricci in the nursery. At first, I didn't want anyone to take care of her, but the nurse assured me she would be okay. I did need to rest -- I couldn't disagree with her. I felt like I had run a marathon, and I was exhausted. Wil stayed with me all night, and he called everyone to tell them the good news. We lay in the hospital bed together thanking the Lord for our blessing. I thought to myself, *I have a baby girl*. As I smiled with joy and delight, I fell asleep in Wil's arms.

Chapter Ten

It seemed like I was standing still, as time was passing me by. I was watching as my marriage with Wil progressed into a more beautiful relationship. Being a mother had its challenges, but it is one of the best times of my life. It was amazing to watch Ricci grow from day to day. I couldn't imagine my life without her. Last I heard of Anthony, he was in jail. The only difference was he couldn't pay off a judge or break out this time around. He was in a maximum security prison outside of Lompoc, CA. Life had been perfect.

Our first wedding anniversary was coming up, and I'm completed elated. It's hard to shop for a man who has everything he wants, but I managed to pick up a nice Rolex watch that I thought he would like. I knew he would get me something nice, but as of late he's been very distracted. He had a lot going on at work. So much, in fact, that he decided to hire an Executive Assistant: Laurel Gates. Every time work is mentioned, Laurel's name comes up at least three or more times in the sentence. Even when he comes home at night, he's on the phone with her. Heck, she's been to our house for dinner more than my friends. She was a cute brunette that looked as if she lived in the gym. I try to look on the bright side. He loves me, not her. But sometimes I can't help wonder what may be going on between them. Our anniversary is in three days, and he hasn't said a word. I decided to call for reinforcements.

"Malova, I need help!"
"What's wrong?" she asked.
"You know our first year anniversary is coming up, right?"
"Yeah."
"Wil hasn't said two words about plans."
"Has it occurred to you that he could have a surprise?"

"I don't think so. He spends most of his time with Laurel."

"Who's Laurel?"

"His new executive assistant."

"Okay, he runs an empire. He needs someone to keep him on top of his game. What's wrong with that?"

"She's beautiful and with a two inch waist. She looks like one of those damn Disney cartoon women. I would prefer if she was an ugly, old hag with a brain."

"Now, I know you don't think that he's cheating on you with her, do you?"

"That's exactly what I'm thinking. If he wasn't, then why does he spend half of his time with her and not me and Ricci?"

"Girl, it's nothing but work."

"I don't think work has anything to do with this."

"What do you want me to do?"

"I don't know yet."

"Girl, you need to stop being insecure."

"I am not insecure!"

"Then why are you trippin'?"

"I don't know," I heard Wil come through the door, "Malova, I'll call you back later. Wil just walked through the door."

"Talk to him."

"I will. Bye!"

Wil placed his briefcase down. He looked very tired. I just stared at him. He plopped on the couch and put his hand over his forehead. He still didn't notice that I was standing in the doorway. Ricci came from her playroom and crawled in the living room. Her eyes were bright, and she started to smile.

"Hi, sweetie," he said. He picked her up. He gave her a big hug and a kiss on the cheek, "Where's mommy?" She pointed towards my direction. I still stood in the doorway, looking as if I was ready to burst into tears. Then he says,

"Mommy looks sad. Do you know why mommy looks sad?" Ricci had a blank look on her face, and then she started crying. Wil picked her up and comforted her.

"How was work?" I asked. I really didn't care, but I didn't want to jump into an argument either.

"It was exhausting. We're trying to open another La Bonita in L.A. Thanks to some great ideas that Laurel came up with, the expansion just might fly without any problems. Laurel is a good assistant. She's better than Zora."

"I liked Zora. She was cool."

"Yeah, so cool that she stole $90,000 from the La Bonita service account."

"Other than that, she was cool."

"Courtni, what's up with you? You're acting kind of strange."

"What are we going to do on our anniversary?"

"Oh, that is coming up soon, isn't it?"

"You forgot about our anniversary? How could you?"

"I didn't forget. I've just been very busy."

"Oh, so you can't take time out from playing with Laurel long enough to think about us? That trick has been all you think about. Laurel this! Laurel that! Laurel's a good worker! Laurel can jump off the Empire State Building and still survive! Laurel! Laurel! Laurel!"

"Where does this negative energy come from? Why are you being so insecure?"

"I am not insecure!"

I ran upstairs to our bedroom and slammed the door. I could hear Wil's footsteps coming up as well. He must have put Ricci in her room first before coming to ours. Next thing you know, he pushed to open the door. I was gathering my pillow and blanket.

"Where are you going?" he asked.

"I'm sleeping in the guest bedroom." I picked up my stuff and was about to leave. Wil clutched my arm and pushed me back onto the bed. He hovered over me.

"No, you're not! Not until you tell me what the problem is."

"You are the problem!"

"What the hell Courtni? What have I done?"

"That's exactly what I'm talking about. It's what you haven't done."

"Courtni, I've been busy."

"Busy doing what?"

"I have a job, Courtni. I have responsibilities and those responsibilities make sure that you and Ricci have everything you want and need!"

"Yeah, you're responsibilities also entail running up behind Laurel all the damn time."

"I cannot believe this!! You actually think that I'm sleeping with Laurel? That's the most stupid thing I've ever heard. One, Laurel is engaged to Yavar Campbell, my father's assistant."

"That doesn't mean shit!"

"Two, I am happily married except when my wife is acting like this. You did the same thing on our honeymoon when that chambermaid liked me. Face it, Courtni! You don't trust me!"

"I don't have to listen to anymore of this."

"Oh yes you do! I have never given you a reason not to trust me. In fact, I've given you every reason to trust me. You need to pray and ask God for peace in your troubled heart and have faith in me!"

"Whatever! This is where I walk out of here!"

"I'm not done! You are so used to men playing you, and we won't even mention your last boyfriend."

"This has nothing to do with nothing to do with Anthony!"

"But this has to do what he did to you. That situation is where all of this is stemming from. He played you, and you think I'm going to do the same thing. If I haven't proven to you that I would never do that, then you're just not going to get it!"

I grabbed my stuff and took it into the guest room. I lay on the bed and started to cry. Was Wil right? I wasn't sure. You would think after we've known each other for just over three years that I would put more faith in him than that.

I stayed awake, tossing and turning. A part of me wanted to go and apologize to him -- just to hear him say, *its okay* and we'd make love. Then I came to the realization that I was being silly and that I need to be in the bed with my husband. I got out of the bed with my pillow and headed towards our bedroom. As I walked along the long corridor, I heard Wil on the phone. I went back to the guest room and picked up the phone. He was talking to a female and it sounded like Laurel.

"I can't keep this up much longer." said Wil.
"We have to. Does she suspect anything?" asked Laurel.
"I don't think so. We got into this crazy argument."
"She'll get over it. Don't worry, Wil. Soon, she'll know the truth. We're still going to go ahead as planned. Meet me at The Sandals. We'll finish this discussion later."

My heart fell to floor. All my suspicions were true. My husband is cheating on me with another woman. I think I would have handled this better if we were just dating. Actually, I wouldn't have. I lay in bed until I cried myself to sleep.

The next day, I called Malova and Varsha over.

"I was right, Malova. Wil's cheating on me with Laurel."

"What?" Malova shouted.

"What makes you think that? How do you know?" asked Varsha.

"I caught them on the phone last night."

"So what? People talk on the phone all the time." said Malova.

"Not at 2:30 A.M. they don't!"

"What were they saying, Courtni?" asked Varsha.

"I can't keep this up much longer. She'll never know. She doesn't suspect anything. I damn near lost my mind when I heard that last night. I fell asleep crying."

"I'm so sorry." Varsha replied.

"I'm not! For all we know, you could be jumping the gun. Wil loves you and we all know this. Wil is the only man that has ever loved you. I have more faith in your husband than you do. At this point, I need more proof than a phone conversation!"

"You're right, Malova. I do need more proof! Varsha, I want you to tape them at The Sandals tonight."

"They're going to The Sandals?" Varsha asked.

"Yes, and I want you to tape them tonight. Malova, I want you to help her in any way you can."

"Okay, but it's only for the satisfaction of proving you wrong. You're being silly Courtni!"

"When the tape is complete, I want you guys to come back here, so we can watch at least half of the tape. This will be my anniversary present for him tomorrow, right along with me filing for divorce."

"Courtni, I still think you're jumping the gun, but I will do this for you."

The hours of the day went by very slowly. At 7:00P.M., Wil came home to change clothes. I didn't say a word to him. All I could see was an adulterer. Before he left, he looked at me with hope in his eyes. "I'll be home a little late; kiss Ricci goodnight for me." I still didn't say a word. He held his head down, and he was out the door.

At 9:30 P.M., Varsha, Greg, Malova and Mike came over.

"Did you tape them?" I asked Varsha.
"Yes, but it's not what you thought." she replied.
"What do you mean?"
"Courtni, they were discussing the surprise party for your anniversary."
"You're lying to me."
"Nope," said Mike, "see for yourself."

He put the tape in the VCR. They were talking about catering, presents, how they were going to get me to the place. I was so embarrassed. I knew that as soon as he got home, I owed him a big apology. As a tear fell, I could hear the front door unlocking. Greg ejected the videotape from the VCR right as Wil came into the Recreation Room.

"What's going on here?" Wil asked.
"Oh, we were just in the neighborhood." replied Greg.
"Yeah, we just wanted to see how Courtni was doing." said Mike.
"We'll be going now. We have some business to attend to and Courtni does too. I'll check on you later." said Varsha.

Everyone said goodnight except Malova. She looked so disappointed in me, and rightfully so. Once everyone was gone, Wil and I were alone in the Recreation Room. Ricci was asleep, so there were no baby noises. Margarette had gone home. We were pretty much alone with only silence as our company.

"I guess I'll go up to our room. I take it that you won't be joining me so, see you in the morning."

He walked over to kiss me, but then changed his mind and went upstairs. I stayed on the couch for a while, trying to find the words to say to him. At midnight, I marched upstairs to the guest room and called Laurel and apologized to her.

"I didn't know that you thought that way." she said.

"Yeah, I seriously thought you were sleeping with my husband."

"I can kind of relate. When Yavar's best friend, Jean, came to visit, I was extremely jealous."

"I'm really sorry I misjudged you."

"Apology accepted. Now, you go in there and make up with your husband. He is a wonderful man."

"I know. Thanks for understanding."

"Sure."

I left the guest room and went into our bedroom. Wil was still awake staring at the ceiling.

"Wil, can we talk?"

"If we are going to argue, then no." he replied.

"I don't think so, but there's something I've got to say. Last night, I heard you talking to Laurel. I got the tail end of the conversation. I seriously thought you were cheating on me."

"Why were you ease-dropping on my phone conversation?"

"Wait, let me finish. After hearing that, I decided that I was going to leave you."

"Oh, that lifts my spirits. Tell me, did you ever think to come to me and ask me about Laurel?"

"Will you shut up and let me finish?"

"Why should I? You have already passed judgment, and it seems like you've made your decision."

"Please, Wil, let me finish what I have to say and hear me out completely without interruptions."

"Courtni, I have never been mad at you, but today is the day."

"I don't blame you; you should be mad at me but may I please finish?"

"Go ahead."

"Now, I called Malova and Varsha over to have you videotaped at the hotel. They did it, but to only find out that you two were planning our anniversary party. I called Laurel to apologize. Now it's my turn to apologize to you."

"I cannot believe what I am hearing from you. Furthermore, you clearly think that you're not insecure?"

"Baby, I'm so sorry. If you stay mad at me, I'll understand." Wil stood and walked towards me. He looked as if he was going to kill me. "Sweetheart, please don't be too mad. I promise I'll never doubt you again." He gave me the same passionate kiss that he gave me on our honeymoon. I was shocked at first, but I fell into it. I put my arms around him, and clenched him tightly.

"You're lucky that I can't resist you," he said staring into my eyes, "I know that I've been avoiding you, and I'm sorry. I should have let you know what was going on."

"If you would have told me, it wouldn't have been a surprise."

"It's definitely not a surprise now. You know all the plans."

"I'll act surprised. I love you, Wil."

"I love you too, Courtni and only you. I don't want you to ever forget that. You are going to have to start trusting me. If you don't, this marriage could turn fatal and end."

"I promise I'll work on it. Now, you say you love me, and only me?"

"You know I do."

"Why don't you show me how much?" I stood and let my nightgown drop to the floor. I was completely naked. Wil pushed me back onto the bed. His eyes were filled with pure delight.

"I thought you'd never ask." he said smiling.

Chapter Eleven

My anniversary party was a huge success. I kept my promise and acted surprised, even though my friends knew that I wasn't. We got some really cool gifts from our family, friends and clients. Nora Kennedy gave us tickets to her next New Year's Eve party that was already sold out. I didn't know which event was better!

As we entered the second year of our marriage, things between Wil and me were almost perfect. Sure we had a fight every now and then, but it was nothing major. Ricci was two years old, and we were entertaining having one more child. I wasn't ready because my career and current clientele were already demanding time away from our daughter. Wil's enterprise continued to grow astronomically. He was a candidate for Forbes Magazine top 500 lists. I just felt that we didn't have the time to dedicate to another child. Wil didn't agree. If it were up to him, I wouldn't work, and I'd stay home with the kids and Margarette.

It was a fall day, and Wil decided to take off work to have a family day. We gave Margarette the day off, since she was about to be a new grandmother. Wil gave her a two-thousand dollar bonus to spend on her daughter and grandchild. While Ricci and Wil were playing hide and seek, there was a knock at the door. I went to the door and there was a lady standing there. She was about 5'5", slender -- borderline anorexic, bleached blonde hair with body piercing everywhere. You could tell that once upon a time, she was sightly, but now she seemed to have let herself go.

"Can I help you?" I asked.
"Yes, I am here to see William, please." she replied.
"May I ask who you are?"

"Francis," Wil said. He was coming downstairs with Ricci in hand. I could not believe it. This was the same woman he told me about so many years ago. I could see why he loved and appreciated me so much. I was an upgrade. "What are you doing here?"

"Hey stranger, how are you?" she started smiling. You could tell she was happy to see him. I was trying to keep my composure, but my body language expressed unhappiness.

"I'm just fine. What are you doing here?"

"Can I talk to you, in private?" Oh no she didn't --

"Anything you need to say to me, you can say it in front of my wife."

"You're wife? Who? This chick?" she pointed to me. I wanted to take that finger and rip it off her hand. How dare she? What is she trying to say? I damn sure look better than her!

"This woman is my wife, Francis. Courtni, this is Francis."

"Nice to meet you," I extended my hand, though I really didn't want to. My attempt to be polite failed, as she looked at my hand and viewed with disfavour. I was trying to smear it in that he was my man, and not hers. I withdrew my hand and I placed it behind my back. I was balling up my fist, just in case I needed to lay her out.

"This was not how he told me this would go." She looked confused. I had a puzzled look on my face. Who was this "he" person she was referring to? Wil just looked pissed off.

"Francis, I am trying to rest and enjoy the day with my family."

"Is this your daughter?" Ricci was looking at Francis frowning. She was a pretty good judge of character. If you were a person on the up and up, Ricci would laugh and play with you. If you were shady in any way, she would frown or sometimes even try to hit you.

"This is our daughter. It was great seeing you, but I can tell you have no real reason for being here."

"I want you back, Wil. I want to work things out."
Alright -- it was time to fight.

"Are you on drugs?" Wil gave Ricci to me. Times like
this I wish Margarette was here. I could tell her to take Ricci
upstairs. I didn't want her to see what was about to go down,
but I wasn't trying to miss anything either.

"I know I messed up, and I am sorry. What we had was
beautiful..."

"Yeah, what we had -- as in past tense! Did you not
hear me say this was my wife and my family?"

"She's nothing but the rebound chick, I can accept
that." I put Ricci down, she was about to witness mommy
clowning today!

"How dare you come to my home --" Francis put her
hand up to cut me off. My eyebrows raise and I could feel
myself getting indignant.

"This house is not your home. It belongs to William and
his father." Did this bitch just correct me?

"No!" Wil stepped in front of me "This is Courtni's
home. She is my wife; therefore, this is her house. You will not
come up in here and disrespect my family."

"Wil I speak for myself --"

"No, this is my fight, Courtni. I let you have your
moment, so let me have mine." Okay, now my husband was
shutting me up. I was already mad, but now I was starting to
get pissed off. He did have a point. In my dealings with
Anthony, I told him to not interfere. He respected my wishes
and backed off. Though I don't want to, I will give him the
same respect. Wil got in Francis' face. I hadn't seen him this
mad since the day he choked Anthony at my mom's house.
"This is my wife; not the rebound chick! It has been six years,
since I walked away from you! Why in the hell are you on our
doorstep with this bullshit?!?"

"I love you."

"I'm closing the door!"

"Wait! You loved me once. I was supposed to be your
wife, not her!"

"Things happen for a reason. If you were meant to be my wife, you would have been. You wouldn't have played all your little games, trying to spend up my money and trying to trap me with a kid that didn't belong to me."

"What was I supposed to do? I was losing you!"

"You were losing me due to your actions."

"You were too busy for me. Your father had you running all over Memphis and Long Beach! I was lonely and I needed to get laid! You and your stupid rule about sex before marriage --"

"If you really loved him, you would have waited for him!" There was no way I was going to let them duke it out and not say anything. "I waited and yeah it was hard, but it was worth it. You should have kept your eyes on the prize."

"You shut the hell up! You're the reason why I lost both the men I loved!"

"What the hell? I'm not the reason for --"

"Courtni, don't even waste your breath. She's not worth it!" Wil stepped back to close the door. I kicked my foot out to the side because I wanted to know what she was talking about.

"What are you talking about?" I placed my hand on my hip. I can somewhat understand about Wil, but she said both the men I loved.

"While Wil wasn't giving up the dick, I met someone. I knew he had a girlfriend, but he was always nagging about her. He promised me that he was going to leave her and be with me. When I came up pregnant, he left me and went back to her. That's why I tried to frame it on you that night we got drunk. My child needed to be taken care of, and I needed a husband!"

"What does this have to do with me?"

"I have a son, and his name is Allen Anthony Merrick!"

"AW HELL NAW!" I walked away from the door and sat on the couch. I knew that Anthony cheated, thanks to Varsha, but I would have never guessed that he got someone pregnant. However, when I think about it, it all makes sense;

the dots are totally connected. Before things got really bad between Anthony and me, he got locked up. He told me it was for parking tickets. I remembered that being true because I had to pay the tickets off in order to get him out of jail. Wil told me that Francis's baby daddy got locked up on purpose to avoid paying child support. Considering how scandalous Anthony is, I could see him purposely getting arrested to avoid it. After that, he didn't work regular jobs; he was hustling to get The Whiz sold to him. I wanted to get mad so bad but a voice in my head was saying, get behind me, Satan! That part of my life is done. I started looking around in the mansion. I looked at my daughter who was still mean mugging Francis at the front door. I could see Wil and Francis arguing, but I couldn't hear what they were saying. I starting thinking, and the voice was right, and that part of my life is over. I have a new life -- a blessed life. God was blessing me before, but the majority of my blessings were being blocked because I was spending too much time focusing on a man that was of the world instead of embracing a man that was of Christ. I have that now with Wil. God always had a window open for me. He now has doors wide open pouring out blessings.

As my anger started to subside, I actually felt sorry for Francis. Here was a broken woman at our door, crying out for help and a relationship. I started praying for her, that the Lord would heal her wounds, and that she will be open to receiving Him in her life. After I finished my prayer, I could hear the conversation that was going on between them.

"How did you find me anyways?" Wil asked.

"I called Anthony's mom and asked her why I haven't seen him lately. She informed me that he got sent back to prison, and this time he wasn't getting out. I went to visit him, and he told me to come here to get my child support money. I had no idea that he knew you, and I had no idea that you had married the woman that Anthony was cheating on with me."

At this point, she was crying. All I could do was shake my head. Ricci started copying off of me and was shaking her head too.

"So basically, you're looking for some money."

"That would help so I can feed Allen, but I want my life back with you!"

"I've never hit a woman in my entire life, and I despise men who hit women. In your case, I'm almost ready to make an exception!"

"Wil I am sorry."

"You need to go back to wherever you came from and focus on raising your son. You were a seasonal person that the Lord placed in my life to learn and to help me discover what I really need and want out of a mate. The lesson has been learned, and He has blessed me with the most amazing woman in the world." He turned around and pointed to me.

"That woman sitting right there has laughed with me, cried with me, had faith in me and is walking in Christ with me. She is a blessing that I would never forsake. Goodbye, Francis!"

He slammed the door in her face, and he came and sat down on the couch next to Ricci and me. I put my arms around him and Ricci crawled in his lap.

"I am sorry you had to witness that." He said, with anger in his eyes.

"I'm fine, but I am sorry you had to go through that."

"It is truly a small world. I would have never thought that Francis' baby's father was Anthony."

"That was, unexpected. He never told me he had a kid. Then again, he knew that if I had found out sooner we would have broken up well before we did."

"I could understand that. Besides, he wasn't trying to take care of Allen. By Francis showing up here like this, it proves he never has. It's men like that who make it hard for brothers like me. I'm up here doing the right thing, and he was populating probably twenty-five percent of Long Beach!"

"You're right. The bum probably never will. You were right about something though."

"What was that?"

"For starters, he does make it hard for other brothers trying to do right. I am thankful for what we have and the difference you have made in my life. Because of you, I believe in love and relationships. God couldn't have blessed me with a better husband and father."

"Awe stop it, you're making me blush."

"Another thing that you were right about, I now believe that she was placed in your life for you to learn a lesson. And to add to that, she was placed in your life to lead us to each other."

"You think?"

"I know. I mean, let's think about it -- we were strangers that first met through Malova. On our official first date, you told me about Francis. Today we discover that Francis was linked to Anthony. All these events were set in motion to guide us to each other. Since we serve a God of free will, it was our choice to choose or deny each other."

"Don't you mean it was your choice? When I met you, I had already chosen you."

"Yeah...okay." He kissed me on the cheek. "Even though some of our events were unfortunate and melodramatic, I believe it was a message letting us know that we were meant to be -- that this was God's plan for us now revealed."

"You turn me on when you talk like that."

"Not in front of the baby."

"I know. I can't help but to wonder though. Where would I be if I never knew you? Would I have taken Francis back?"

"Let's not waste our time trying to figure that out."

We looked down and Ricci had fallen asleep. We both walked upstairs and laid her in bed. Wil grabbed my hand and led me to our bedroom. He looked at me and whispered in my ear, "I want you." We slowly undressed and made love until Ricci woke up.

Chapter Twelve

The years went by fast. Ricci was already starting first grade. Wil and I have been married for five and a half years. We've been thinking about having another child, but right now we haven't made a firm decision. However, we've had plenty of fun with target practice. Malova and Mike had two kids, Quincy and Harriett. Varsha and Greg had five kids: The twins Kevin and Tevin, Brenda, Sade', and Rubin. Everything in my life was at peace...until I got a disturbing phone call from Anthony.

"It's been a long time, Courtni." he said.

"What do you want, Anthony?" I wasn't in the mood for bullshit today.

"Remember when I said that you were gonna pay Courtni?"

"That was over five years ago. Get to the point so I cannot only continue with my day, but also deliberate on if I'm going to call the police. I believe this phone conversation is in violation of your restraining order."

"You are in no position to threaten me. It's time to pay the check."

"Now here you go with your empty threats. Before I hang up the phone, I want to know what I have done to you to make you hate me so much. You are the one who caused me grief!"

"You've ruined my life, you selfish little bitch! First, you embarrassed me in front of Tasha at that restaurant..."

"Are you still on that? That's old news. Have you heard the term of let go and let God? Did you find Jesus during your time of being away?"

"We had something good going. She was definitely wife material! After that night, she didn't want anything to do with me. Second, you had me arrested. I've been in here for five years now. I haven't seen daylight for a long time. This is something that isn't easy to get over, and don't think I'm not trying."

"I'm sure you are. By the way, how's your son Allen doing?"

"So Francis had guts to show up, I see. How did you like my present?"

"It didn't faze me one bit -- just confirmed a lot of things. But I will tell you one thing, I forgive you Anthony."

"You what?"

"Yeah, I forgive you. I forgive all the lies and deceit you created in our relationship. I forgive you for the physical and mental abuse you caused me. Foremost, I thank you for the chain of events you set in motion that led me to my husband and my family."

"I didn't ask for your forgiveness. You can take that and shove it up your ass! All I want is revenge! I get out in three months, and I will get it."

"Aren't you tired of threatening me, Anthony?"

"No, it's a promise."

"Oh, I am so worried."

"You better be."

After that, there was a click. Was he really serious? If he is, oh well. Anthony Merrick's threats don't scare me anymore. At 3:30 P.M., I had to go and pick up Ricci from school. Wil had to work late as usual, so I had to do it. While we were in the car, Ricci asked me a very disturbing question.

"Mommy," she says," who is Uncle Tony?"

"Sweetheart, there is no Uncle Tony."

"Yes there is. He said he was Uncle Tony. He's in prison, and he said when he gets out, he is going to come and visit me."

"Oh dear." My heart fell to the floor. I knew Anthony had called my little girl, but how? How did he even know her name? What school she went to? Was he going to take his revenge upon my baby? I was so scared. "Honey, when did this man call you?"

"He called during lunch. Is he going to hurt me, Mommy?"

"No, sweetheart, he's not going to harm you, me or your daddy, ever."

I pulled up in our driveway, and dropped Ricci off with Margarette. I kissed her goodbye, and I was off to Wil's office. I parked the car in a no parking zone, rushed up the elevator, and into his office. His secretary was at the desk.

"May I help you?" she asked.

"I'm here to see William Masterton." I said out of breath.

"Do you have an appointment?"

"I'm his wife. I don't need an appointment!"

"It's all right, Marge," Wil interrupted coming out of his office, "She is my wife. Come in, honey." I rushed in his office. I had tears in my eyes. I was literally crying like a baby. "Courtni, sweetheart, what's wrong?"

"Oh dear God! He's going to live up to his threat!"

"Who?"

"Anthony! He called and while I was helping Margarette and...."

"Slow down," he took me in his arms, and wiped my tears with his hand, "and tell me calmly and slowly."

"Anthony called the house today, and said he was going to live up to his threat. I really ignored him, but he called Ricci at school today. He said he was Uncle Tony, and he was going to come and see her. I think he just might try and take her. He's going to try to hurt my baby."

"He is not going to hurt any of us...."

"He knew I was pregnant but how did he find out her name? The school? I'm so confused and scared!"

"It's all right, darling. Unfortunately, I think he probably found out her name from Francis. I could see her doing, that since I wouldn't take her back, nor give her money to help with their son."

"That worthless...."

"I'm coming home with you. We are going to talk to Ricci together. Let me get my things." He grabbed his suitcase and locked up his desk. He took my hand and led me out of his office. "Marge! Tell everybody that I'm taking off for the rest of the day. Have Laurel get my notes and conduct the board meeting in my absence."

She came into the office with a puzzled look on her face, "But sir, what about the meeting?"

"Forget the meeting! I have a very important matter to attend to at home. I trust Laurel to take care of things in my absence."

"But sir, this could expand your corporation and...."

"Do you like your job, Marge?"

"Yes sir."

"Do you want to remain working here?"

"Yes sir, but —"

"Then I suggest you never question me or my orders again. Now, get out of my way."

She moved over to the side, and we passed her. She gave me a cold, dirty look, but at the time I didn't care.

We arrived at home a short time later. I was still shaking; tears and cold sweat were leaving my body, because I knew he was going after my little girl.

"Margarette," said Wil, "go and get Ricci for me. Courtni and I have to talk to her."

"Yes sir." she replied.

She ran upstairs to get her. Ricci was slowly coming down the stairs; she had a puzzled look on her face.

"Am I in trouble, Daddy?"

"No, sweetie."

"Then what is it? Why is Mommy crying?"

"She's just upset because this man called you. We don't have an Uncle Tony in our family. There's only Uncle Malik, Gustavo, Mike and Greg."

"Who is Tony then, Daddy?"

"He's a very bad man who tried to hurt Mommy a long time ago. He almost killed you when Mommy was carrying you."

"Then, he's a bad man?"

"Yes honey, and if he ever calls you again, don't accept his phone call. In fact, I'm going to call your principal and tell him if it isn't me or your mother, then don't call you to the office for the phone."

"Okay Daddy. No more talking to the bad man."

"Now go upstairs, and get ready for dinner."

Ricci fled upstairs. When she was half way up, she came back down to me. "Don't cry, Mommy. Everything will be fine." She kissed me on the cheek and gave me a big hug. I hugged her back, and she went back up the stairs. I started pacing the floor in the living room.

"Everything is going to be alright," said Wil, "You'll see."

"I'm going to visit him tomorrow before I go to pick up Ricci. Something feels very wrong about all this."

"Courtni, I don't think that's very wise."

"Well I don't care about being wise right now. All I want is for him to leave me alone. I think it's so childish that he's carrying this teenage grudge. It's been almost nine years, since we broke up, Wil. All I want is for this ordeal to end."

"I understand. However, you have to think this out rationally. You might be playing into his hands by visiting him."

"That may be true but I need to get to the bottom of this, for our family's sake."

"You're right. At least allow Malik or Gustavo to go with you. I'd prefer if both accompany you."

"That's fine. I'll allow either or both."

"Good. Be careful, honey."

"I will. I love you so much. I am so sorry that my past won't stay where it belongs."

"I never want you to think this is your fault. Anthony is the crazy person—not you. As long as we are together, there's nothing or no one that can stand in your way of being happy."

"William Sloan Masterton, I love you more than anyone could ever know or feel."

"And I love you, Courtni Renee' Taylor-Masterton. You know, you have too many names."

"Yeah," I started chuckling. Wil wiped the last tear from my eye. "I guess I do. Let's go to bed."

The next morning came quickly. It didn't seem like I went to bed at all, probably because Wil and I made love all night long. I did my usual when I got up: took Ricci to school and helped Margarette around the house. At 2:00 P.M., I decided to go and see Anthony. He was in the local prison in Lompoc. I kept my promise and called Malik and Gustavo. Malik was still working on his new case, so Gustavo accompanied me. When I told the guard who I came to see, I got the shock of my lifetime.

"Mr. Merrick was released today for good behavior." said the guard.

"What?" I replied.

"Yep. He was my little pet. That man did everything I told him to do. It also helped that he wrote the judge every month telling him about his progress."

"Who authorized his release?" asked Gustavo, "When I checked the records at the precinct, they clearly stated that he was not up for release for six months or so."

"The judge called an early parole hearing. After Merrick gave his statement, the judge had a soft heart, so he let him go during his parole hearing."

"Sounds to me that he's managed to pay off another judge or maybe even the warden of this prison. He's done this type of thing before to get an early release."

"Sir, that's not my problem."

"It will be your problem! Do you know what you have done?"

"What do you mean?"

"Yesterday he called me threatening my life. He called my daughter at school terrifying her."

"With all due respect ma'am, I don't think Mr. Merrick would jeopardize his freedom so soon."

"Well with all due respect sir, you don't know Anthony Merrick like I do."

"With all due respect, guard, you don't know Anthony at all!" shouted Gustavo.

"What is your name again?"

"Courtni Masterton."

"Wow! I feel like I'm meeting a celebrity. You're the reason why he got sent here. He talked about you all the time—about how sorry he was fir all the things that he put you through. You know he still love you."

"Whatever. The only thing that Anthony loves is himself. Furthermore, I disagree with that. He's the reason why he got sent here."

"Well, in any case he mentioned you in all his letters to the judge saying that the first thing he was going to do is give a personal apology to you for ruining your life and sanity."

"You and the judge bought all that crap?"

"Well, he did sound convincing ma'am."

"Then you're a fool," stated Gustavo, "and I am going to make sure your warden hears about this. You will lose your job!"

"Why? What did I do?"

"You seem a little too sweet on Merrick! I also think it's rather funny that Merrick knew about my niece and where her school was. You would or could gain access to that information through police and public record files. Oh yeah, buddy -- someone is going down, and I am starting with you!"

"I got to go to my daughter. Let's go, Gustavo."

We ran out of the prison and towards my car. As I drove down the highway heading back to Long Beach, my heart was racing almost as fast as the cars racing around me. Neither speed limits nor laws of the land were of importance to me. Luckily, Gustavo drove his car as well, and he had his sirens on behind me. Even if Gustavo wasn't with me, I had to get to my Ricci! When I arrived at the school, cops were everywhere. Wil was waiting outside. By the look on his face, I could tell I was too late.

"He took her." said Wil.

"I'm going to kill him. If he touches one hair on my child, I will kill him."

"I thought he was getting out in six months?"

"I just came from the prison. They gave him an early release for good behavior."

"Playing the role for early release."

"Pretty much," said Gustavo, "More like paying for early release. He had help from one of the local guards. He was the one who told us that he got out today. I think he had a lot to do with it."

"I can't believe this is happening after all this time." I started to cry, "This is my fault...it is...it's...."

"You can't blame yourself for everything malicious he does!" Wil shouted, "We need to focus our energy on getting our daughter back and not worrying about how, why and when Anthony Merrick does the things he does."

"What do we do?"

"He left this note."

I took the letter in my hands. I couldn't hold it still because I was so angry.

My Dearest Courtni,

This is just the beginning. The cycle is only on wash. You thought I was joking, did you? Now who's tough? Now who has the power? Ricci is very pretty. She has your eyes and your new temper. I almost didn't get her. Trust me, it wasn't easy. I had to kill her teacher, and one of her classmates for attempting to be heroic. I don't mind because you're not going to say a word to the police. I have inside contacts, so I'll know if you said anything. I paid some nice money for an early release, so I can't go back to jail just yet. I'm up to my old tricks, and I've got brand new ones in the bag. If you and Robin Hood love your precious little girl, my name had better not come up, or she dies.

I could feel the blood rushing through my head. Heat seemed to have consumed my entire body. I know Wil said this wasn't my fault, but I couldn't let go of the fact that he is my ex. He was my bad dating choice, and because of that choice, my daughter is now in danger. All I could think about was my baby. The vision of her face and the sound of her laughter consumed me. Then his voice in my ear and picturing him with her was killing me. I have to find him, and I have to save her. In addition, when I do find him, I will kill him.

Chief Marton came up behind me and touched me on my shoulder.

"Mrs. Masterton, we are going to do everything in our power to find your daughter. This bastard killed her teacher and a ten-year-old boy. If there is anything you want to tell me, let me know."

"Sir, I want to be on this case." said Gustavo.

"You can count me in as well." said Malik. He had just come back from the school. He must have stopped by an armory on his way to the house because he had guns all over his body, like, he was ready for war. "This punk has my niece! He just doesn't know he has messed with the wrong family."

"Boys, I don't think it's a good idea." replied the Chief.

"With all due respect sir, we are going to be on this case with or without your permission." stated Malik.

Chief Marton replied, "You're too close to the situation—"

"This is why we are working this case. We'll keep our cool. I know how to make the justice system work me." stated Gustavo.

"There is something we need to tell you, Chief Marton." said Wil.

"No!" I shouted. My instincts were telling me that we needed to play by Anthony's rules – for the moment.

"What is going on?" asked Chief Marton.

"I need to speak with my husband alone for a moment."

"Ma'am, I encourage you to be up front with us as we are all on the same side. If you attempt to take the law into your own hands you could put your daughter in more danger than she already is."

"Like I said, Chief, I need to speak to my husband alone, please!"

I pulled Wil over to the side. He grabbed me by the waist and pulled me close to his ear for us to whisper.

"Are you crazy?" Wil asked.

"At this point, I just might be. Anthony's got our kid." I replied.

"Baby, the chief is right. We need to work with them."

"Did you read that note carefully?"

"Yes, but what does that have to do with anything?"

"Did you notice the part when he said he had inside contacts?"

"Yeah, but I'm not taking what that note said at face value."

"Damn it, you better. He's got my baby and I delivered her right to him."

"Courtni, that's not true."

"The hell it isn't. Let's think about this, the phone call I got yesterday was to throw us off, and it worked. Considering he knew where she went to school, he's not lying about the inside connections, And quite frankly I think that guard Gustavo spoke to today is one of them. I'd rather play it safe and do what Anthony says for right now. That guard gave us some distinctive hints that he knew what Anthony was up to."

"Can we at least talk to Marton privately at home or something? I know the Chief, and he's a good man. He and my father grew up together, and he has had nothing but my family's best interest at heart. Let's not forget he got the restraining order against Anthony in affect forty-eight hours after I called him. You should know by now that we can trust him."

"I don't trust him. At this point, I trust no one!"

"You always refer to Ricci as your baby. Well, she's mine too, and I do have some say in this, and in her life. I know I haven't been the perfect father, but I try to be."

"You're right. I'm sorry. And you're a great father. I'm just angry and scared. I think I'm losing it all at once."

"I am too, but we will get through this together. In fact, I'll even compromise. I'll talk to Marton and tell him in order for us to give him information on this note; he has to allow Malik and Gustavo to be on the case."

"That is a fair compromise. Let's go with that plan."

We told Chief Marton to meet us at seven o'clock at our home and to come only with Malik and Gustavo. When they arrived, I told them the situation, and showed them the letter.

He understood our situation and hesitantly accepted our terms.

"They may still need a back up officer to cover this." said the Chief.

"I don't think so," I replied, "I've seen Malik and Gustavo handle Anthony before they became a part of Long Beach's Finest. They can handle him with no problem."

"Alright, but I want you boys playing by the rules. No gangster methods with this."

"Yes sir!" they replied.

"Gustavo has already connected the phone tap. I suspect he'll be calling tonight."

"I hope so," Wil continued," I want to give him a big piece of my mind and..." The phone rang. Wil was the closest, so I agreed that he should be the one to talk to him first. I was in no frame of mind to speak to him now. Thoughts of lunging a knife through Anthony's body was all I could think of.

The Chief signaled for Wil to pick up the phone.

"Hello."

"William. Oh William. There's someone who's dying to talk to you."

I knew it was Anthony. Wil held the phone with anger. I could see the veins popping out of his neck. I signaled for him to put the phone on speaker.

"Daddy?" It was my baby. Thank God she was safe.

"Ricci! Are you alright?"

"Yes. You were right about Uncle Tony. He is mean!"

"Has he done anything to hurt you?"

"No, but he says I have to go now. There are some things he has to discuss with Mommy."

"Wil, put your darling wife on the phone." said Anthony.

"I want my child back. I want my child back now!"

"Temper! Temper! Is that anyway to talk to a man who has your daughter's life in his hands."

"I don't give a damn about my temper! You listen and you listen well. My wife and I have been living a peaceful life without you in it. What happened between you and us years ago is ancient history. We've gotten on with our lives. We don't give a damn about you. All we want is Ricci back safe in our arms."

"That can be easily arranged. I'll make a deal with you since you seem to have reason about you. I want $150 million and half of everything you own. Clear?"

"Are you really that insane? Do you know that you can go right back to jail on kidnapping charges? Even if I did agree, you'd be free and rich for less than twenty-four hours before you are right back in the slammer!"

"This is why I specified in my note that no police involvement is allowed. I won't get locked up unless you tell, and if you were that stupid, then your daughter dies. Now, are we clear?

"Clear, but I want my child back tonight."

"I'll give her back. Be at the Pier twelve midnight, and remember, none of Long Beach's finest."

"You have a deal."

After that, there was a click.

"You're not going to give him the money are you?"

"No," said Chief Marton, "Wil did exactly what I wanted him to do. Hey Malik! Did you get the address?"

"Yes sir. 6253 Sunset Hills Blvd." said Malik.

"Courtni, that's your old house. Doesn't Deidra live there?" asked Wil.

"Yeah, but I have a good notion of where he has her -- the basement. Deidra has always had a fear of the basement. If she hears a noise down there, she won't go to check it out. She's at work right now anyway. There's a passage on the side of the house that leads to the basement. Before Anthony and I officially started dating, we used to go down there and make out. My parents never liked him, so I had to keep our messing around a secret. He knows where the passage is and how to get in."

"We'll go right now." replied Chief Marton.

We all hopped in the van and went to my family home. Wil, Gustavo and I went to the passage. The Chief and Malik went to the front door. I pushed open the brick, and I saw Anthony sitting next to Ricci. She was tied up in a chair with tape over her mouth. Wil jumped inside and charged after Anthony. He threw him over the table and placed his hands around his throat. While Wil was choking Anthony, I untied Ricci. She was surprised to see me and gave me a big hug. The Chief and Malik came down the stairs. Both had an eerie look on their faces.

"I'm gonna kill you!" Wil was shouting.

"William, get off of him." said The Chief. "Malik, get your friend!"

"I'm not ain't touching him," replied Malik, "he is lucky he's gotten to him before me. I'd have shot his ass!"

"Gustavo?"

"I don't want to, but I don't want my boy to go down for murder." said Gustavo. He walked over to Wil. I could hear Anthony barely coughing, and it sounded like his breathing was labored. Wil was really killing Anthony. Gustavo placed his hands on Wil's shoulder, "Let him go man. He isn't worth you going to jail over. I want you to do this, but bigger picture; he isn't worth going to hell over either."

"He is mine!"

"Think about your family, man. Think about your salvation and you standing before Christ. Jesus wouldn't be proud, dawg."

"Courtni, can't you control him?" asked the Chief.

"Nope -- not at all, I want to kill him myself. If Wil wasn't over there doing it, I'd do it, but I'd stab him."

"I understand that you are both upset, but think about what baby girl is looking at right now!" stated Gustavo. Baby girl was his nickname for Ricci, "Think about how I will have no choice but to let the Chief arrest you when you kill him! Courtni, think about raising baby girl without your beloved. Anthony will go back to jail, and he will stay there. I don't care what connections that worthless slime has. He will never bother your family again! You know I'll make sure of it!"

"Wil, he's right." I thought about what Gustavo said. I'd rather have my husband home with us then hugging him from a jail cell. "Killing him won't prove a thing. You'll just end up going to jail and proving that Anthony has the power over us. As much as I hate to say this, but we cannot let him win! I love you, and I need you at home. Not behind bars."

Wil let him go, but I could tell in his eyes that he really didn't want to. Honestly, I didn't want him to, but this was the best course of action. As Wil backed away from him, Anthony staggered to his feet and jumped out the window. Malik ran after him. I went up to Wil and hugged him.

"Are you okay?"

"I'm fine," he replied, "I just lost it for a minute."

"I lost him." said Malik running back in the basement a few minutes after.

"You what? How could you lose him?"

"We'll put out a warrant for his arrest. We have enough evidence to keep him in jail this time."

We all went home, not saying a word. Margarette put Ricci to bed, and left shortly afterwards. I started pacing around our bedroom. I couldn't believe that Anthony got away. I had hope that all of this would be finally over, but it seemed that he was right: this was only the beginning. I looked over at Wil – lying across the bed. He looked very calm.

"I can't believe he got away!" I screamed.

"A part of me wishes that I would have gone ahead and killed him. In the end, I'm glad I didn't. All things will be put in their rightful place."

"What do you mean? Why do you sound so cryptic suddenly?"

"I just have faith – that's all my love." Wil got off the bed and walked towards me. He unbuttoned my shirt – exposing my breast. I was frightened, yet turned on at the same time.

"How in the hell can you think of sex at a time like this?" He continued taking off my clothes.

"I can't explain it, but I want you. I want you right now. I want to kiss away your fear. I want to stroke away your pain. Let me lose myself inside your love."

I was instantly turned on. His hands grasped my hips; his fingers started adventuring the lower parts of my body. I opened my legs and started moaning. My hands traveled to his erection. I started stoking him slowly. Wil whispered his affections in my ear. He lifted me, and carried me to the bed. My worried and fear faded away as his head was in between my spread legs. His tongue was rapidly flicking back and forth across my fleshly lips. He came up and placed his erection inside me. The both of us uttered wordless moans as we made love all through the night. The kisses were more passionate. Feeling him inside of me made my body more excited and tingly. Every thrust was more powerful than the previous. I climaxed repeatedly, with every orgasm being almost too much to handle --, but at the same time I didn't want him to stop. I wanted this love making to last a lifetime, but somehow I knew it wouldn't. It felt like it was our last time. Both of us were still awake, so I decided to talk to him.

"Words can't describe what that was."

"It was a powerful moment – in deed." he replied.

"Why do you look so puzzled now? Do you now feel what I was feeling before our pleasure episode?"

"Not at all. I still feel peaceful. I just know that this will all be over – very soon. Anthony won't bother you anymore."

"Don't you mean us?"

"Oh yes."

"I guess I'll try to go to sleep then."

"Can I hold you in my arms?"

"Of course. You know that you don't have to ask me that."

"I love you, Courtni. I've loved you from the first moment I saw you standing at the pier with your friends. I'll love you until my last breath and even beyond the grave."

"I love you too, baby. Why are you talking like that?"

"I just wanted you to know."

The next day went by slowly. I kept Ricci out of school, and Wil was called away for a short meeting. We had mother/daughter quality time at the park. It was rather fun seeing her laugh and play. After we got home, I put Ricci to bed myself that night.

"Did you have fun today, sweetie?"

"Yes ma'am. Can we go to the circus tomorrow?"

"Of course we can."

"Can daddy go too?"

"Yep, because daddy has the whole day off tomorrow. That's why he went to work today. "

"Cool. Goodnight Mommy."

"Sleep tight sweetheart."

I kissed her on the cheek and left. The phone was ringing so I went to answer it.

"Hello." I said.

"Hey Courtni, its Malik."

"Hey, what 's going on ?"

"A tip. The bartender from La Bonita just called here. It seems that Merrick was following Wil. He said Merrick had ten tequila shots and three beers. When Merrick asked for a fourth beer, the bartender refused to serve him anymore. He made a statement, saying that Anthony went on and on about revenge, so he called me ASAP. When Anthony started to leave, the bartender tried to stop him, but was unable to. He was leaving just as Wil was leaving."

"Malik, what are you saying to me?"

"I've called for reinforcements. Gustavo is on his way to your house because Merrick is out for blood. I think he's going to try and attack Wil while he's drunk."

I heard an explosion outside.

Chapter Thirteen

I ran outside and saw fire and smoke everywhere. I approached closer to the scene to see Wil's car and Anthony's motorcycle. Looking into the distance I saw Anthony's body; it must have been thrown from the accident. A part of me was thinking to myself, I hope you die, bastard. In the midst of the blaze I heard coughing. Over to my right, I saw Wil trying to climb out of a flame engulfed car. I ran over to him as quickly as I could. I didn't care about the fire or smoke. All I wanted was my husband.

"Baby, I got to get you out of here. All this smoke and gas the car is bound to further explode." I was screaming to him.

"Courtni, get out of here. I don't want you to get hurt." Wil replied.

"I am not leaving without you."

"Where's Anthony?"

"Damn Anthony! All I care about is getting you out of this car before it goes up. I cannot lose you. I will not let him take you away from me."

"You will never lose me. My heart will be with you always -- no matter what. You have to promise me that you will raise Ricci to be just as strong and beautiful as you are."

"Stop talking like that! You will be around to see what Ricci becomes."

"I pray that you're granted peace over time. I've lived a great life, Courtni. I'm thankful that you've been a part of it."

"Stop it! I'm getting you out."

"Whether you like it or not, this is my time. I wouldn't exchange one moment in my life. Be strong because Ricci will need your strength. I love you, Courtni."

I was stubborn and determined to get Wil out of the car. As hard as I pulled, I wasn't able to budge him. I started hearing clicking noises. I continued pulling on him until a great force knocked me out the way. As I was sent flying away from Wil's car, I saw an angelic figure standing behind the car with his arms extended – almost as if he pushed me out the way. There was a final click and then another explosion. I watched Wil's car scatter all over the street. In the distance, I heard the alarm from the fire trucks. The blaze started covering Wil's face until I could see him no more. I started screaming uncontrollably. Suddenly, I felt weak and dizzy. Everything was spinning: the house, the last moment seeing Wil's face, Anthony's motorcycle -- until everything went black.

"I think she's trying to come to."
"Poor dear; to watch her husband burn to death, this must have taken a toll on her."
"Her body couldn't handle it, which is why she passed out. I think her eyes are opening. There's definitely movement. Nurse! I need water…stat!"

My body ejected upwards. My eyes were blinded by bright white lights. When I regained my focus, I saw doctors, nurses, the Chief, Malik and Gustavo. They all had sad looks on their faces. I knew they were all sad about Wil, but I think they were more bothered about the fact that I watched him die. The silence and their stares felt like eternity. I sat there in silence pondering over my life with Wil. I know we live to die, but my time with him was so short. I wanted to be mad at God, but I couldn't bring myself to form anger against him. If it wasn't for him, I would have never met Wil at all. My sense of benevolence was escaping me. Though I have family and friends to support me through my time of suffering, I still felt empty. My soul feels lost – wandering around in darkness. What awoke me from my trance were thoughts of Anthony. I was eager to know his fate.

"Courtni, I'm so sorry about Wil." said Malik.

"It's not your fault."

"I feel like it is. Ever since I could remember, Wil has always been there for me. He was like a brother to me. I should have protected him more -- knowing that Anthony was going to be after him."

"You did your best, Malik. I do not blame you for this. Besides, I could talk to him before the car exploded. He said it was his time, and I believed him. With that being said, no one could have prevented this from happening. I think all of us would have preferred, he died a different way, but fate saw different. Speaking of fate, I need to know about Anthony. Is he dead?"

"No, but he is in critical condition."

"What?!?"

"Don't worry about him. If he does make it out of this alive, he will never see the light of day." said the Chief, "In fact, my office is pushing for the death penalty on this one. There's nothing anyone will be able to do. Not even his hook-ups in prison will be able to get him off of this one. I have made sure of it already."

"How is that?"

"Well, that security guard that he managed to pay off and was doing all of those favors for is now unemployed. Gustavo was right in his hunch. He fed Anthony as much information about your family as he could. The Warden of Lompoc has been fired as well. It seems that his daughter used to date Anthony and that is how he got off. So, as you can see, things have been taken care of."

"That's not good enough! I want to see him!"

"Courtni, I do not think that would be a good idea."

The hospital room door flung open; it was my friends. Varsha came over and gave me a big hug. Mike held my hand. Malova stood over in the corner with a look of vengeance in her eyes. Our eyes connected and we both nodded our heads.

She was thinking the same thing I was. It was time for Anthony to die.

"I'll be fine, Malik. I won't do anything stupid."

Malova helped me off the bed. As my feet hit the floor, I became dizzy and started clutching my stomach. There was a sharp pain, like someone was stabbing my insides.

"Courtni, what's the matter?" asked Malova.

"I don't know. Something with my stomach."

"You need to relax and get rest. The shock of losing your husband has taken a toll on your pregnancy." stated the nurse.

"Pregnancy? You've got to be kidding."

"No ma'am. You didn't know?"

"No. I had no idea. This is not the time. I can't handle this right now."

"You'll be just fine, Mrs. Masterton. Now I think your friend, and I should help you back to bed."

"No, don't touch me. I am going to see Anthony."

"You heard her," said Malova, "I will help her to Mr. Merrick's room. She will be okay with me by her side."

As I walked down the hall of the hospital, I saw my soul returning to me, but it was dark. As I walked towards the white, fiery sphere with the blackened centered, I saw images of the past few years pertaining to my life with Wil and Anthony: The pains of Anthony Merrick; the hesitation I felt when I first spoke to Wil; the joy I felt when we fell in love. I felt as if all of that has had been taken away from me, like my life had purpose, but now the purpose has been redefined in a way that's displeasing. I wanted Anthony to agonize -- agonize like I did when we broke up -- agonize like I did when he kidnapped Ricci; and agonize like I am right now. My husband is gone and it's his fault. In the end, this really may have been Wil's fate, like he told me before he died. I also believe that fate can be different. He didn't have to die like that -- not by Anthony's hands.

We approached Anthony's room slowly. There he was lying in his bed with machines hooked up all around him. The left side of his face was burned. The heart monitor was faint, but he was still alive. I approached his bed while Malova stood on the other side of the bed. His eye opened and he saw me. He formed a smirk on his face.

"I got him," he said softly, "I know I did."
"Yeah, you did. Are you happy now? I am suffering!"
"I've only begun to make you suffer. This is only the beginning. I heard you're pregnant again."
"How did you --"
"I heard the nurse talking about it to another nurse. They said that your baby's in danger as well. Because of all the stress of this situation, you are in a fragile state, and if you are not in a calm state you will miscarry. I'd love to make that happen."
"You won't be able to make much of nothing happen. See, if you survive this you'll be going back to prison, and you won't get out. You may even get the death penalty."
"Is that so? Ha! I highly doubt it."
"This time, Anthony I wouldn't."
"You underestimate me and my connections. Chief Marton may have removed some obstacles, but I still have recruits on the course. I may do some more time, but I'll never get the death penalty. And once again, when I get out, I will be after you."
"Well if that's the case, then I'll make sure you won't get out."
"Really? How do you plan to do that?"
" I'm going to watch you die and then walk away."

I went to grab the plugs from the hospital equipment, but Malova grabbed me head. She shook her head no, and kicked the plugs to all his machines. Beeping noises surrounded the room. Anthony started coughing and gasping for air. I reached for his IV, and he grabbed my hand.

"What the fuck do you think you're doing?" he declared.

"Ending my misery known as you. You've been nothing but fatal in my life, and now you've been fatal to my marriage."

"This is murder! You won't get away with this!"

"Who cares?" said Malova, "Your death will not be on her conscious or her hands. It will be on mine. You've damaged my life as well. Daidus could have been so much more if you hadn't interfered with his life. You are a destroyer of life, and it's about time for you to be destroyed."

"Goodbye, Anthony."

Those were the last words I uttered before Malova grabbed my hand to leave the room. I heard the flat line. At last, Anthony Merrick was gone.

Epilogue

It's been six years since I've picked up my journal, and I realized the last entry was after I got home from the hospital the night that William and Anthony died. Afterwards I went through somewhat of a tough time emotionally, but now I am in a better place to talk about the aftermath.

Arranging Wil's funeral was difficult, but I was so thankful to have the friends that I have. They saw that everything was taken care of. The ending product was nice and peaceful. All services were held at our church by the mansion. Though it was sad, I could still feel blessings and love being shared with all who attended.

At the grave site, Wil's parents were broken up. Sloan is an extremely proud man, but I learned that day that even the strongest men can cry. To look at him resting is head on his wife shoulders; tears falling like a waterfall I myself couldn't help but weep....not only for my pain and suffering, but for his as well. Mrs. Masterton was such a puissant and compassionate woman. She stroked Sloan's hair and planted kisses on top of his head. You could tell that her time for tears would come much later, as she felt that it was time to be strong for her husband that day. I love them both so much, and I am thankful to have them in my life as extended family. As a parent you never think about laying your child to rest. It's typically imagined the other way around.

Ricci took it the hardest, as she was truly a daddy's girl. This will be her last year going through spiritual counseling at our church. On her twelfth birthday, she will start confirmation classes to study the importance of worship, prayer and evangelism. This was a decision she made on her on. I am so proud of her. To look at her every day, I see William. Even though he's gone from this world I see him through the eyes of my children -- especially Ricci. The six years of counseling seemed to work, but sometimes I wonder though....is she putting on a front? Is she showing me things that I want to see? Saying things I want to hear? Ricci tells me often that she doesn't want me to worry, but as a mother I can't help it. She still spends a lot of time in her room with the door closed. When I walk in, she's lying in bed, staring at the wall. The same little girl that was afraid to go down a slide is now the pre-teen that climbs trees, skateboards and loves to go skydiving with Malik and Gustavo. I may be overreacting, but I just find it....odd....

I had mild complications with Angelus -- mainly because I was under a lot of stress, as well as experiencing great depression. I now look at my sweet boy as he runs around the mansion. I named him Angelus in honor of the angelic spirit that shielded us from the blast. He knew of Angelus existence – even though I did not. I believe that spirit was sent from the Lord to protect us, and he continues to do so. Angelus use to ask about his father and why he isn't around. There were times when all I could do was cry. With Malik and Gustavo's assistance, he knows who his father was. Earlier in the year, I took Angelus to his father's grave. It was impressive to watch him talk to his father like he was actually there. It was at that time I experienced the peace that I have now. Through Angelus, Wil is still very much with me as well as my guardian angel. Like the Angel who came to Mary announcing she was chosen to carry Christ -- Angelus came to me giving me peace about Wil's death.

As for Anthony's funeral, or lack thereof, it consisted of a pine box with an unmarked grave behind the Lompoc County jail. His own mother didn't even attend. Daidus said that Francis came crying on his doorstep begging him to go with her to view the grave. After that situation with Jimma, their relationship fell off. After Daidus recovered from his injuries from Jimma, he told me that he found the money Jimma was looking for in an old coffee can at his house. Daidus used the stash to set up a trust fund for Allen. He told me when he came to Wil's funeral that he felt it was only right, since Anthony did nothing for his own son. Daidus made sure that the trust fund was in Allen's name only -- Francis was not allowed to touch it. I'm pretty sure that pissed her off.

Though I still experience sadness from time to time, and I miss my Wil terribly, I have much to live for. As I sit and recap the most intimate details of my life, I realized that my life has not taken a turn for the worst. Sure there were trials, but in the end I am still blessed. I have two beautiful reminders of the best days of my life. Anthony played a small, but yet big part of my life. He represented everything in a man that I didn't want or need. He may have been the most damaging relationship in my life, but it was also a blessing in the end. What Wil set out to do in the beginning of our relationship was done, and this was a lesson well learned. If Anthony hadn't hurt me so much before William came along, I would not have been able to appreciate the man that would later be my husband and the father of my children. My soul is at peace, and I can move forward with my life knowing these things and praising God along the way.

The interesting part about all of this is, if I could do it all over, I wouldn't change a thing. Well....Anthony would have died sooner.

THE END

About the Author

Born and raised in St. Louis, Missouri, Alicia Rice has been writing short stories, poetry and novels since the earlier childhood. Raised in a loving family by her grandmother and aunt, Alicia grew up in home surround by love and creativity. Fatal Marriage was originally written April 21, 1994 and has been a growing work of art over the years. Though this novel is fictional, Alicia brings her personal experiences alive through the pages of her book which reflects her inner strength in life. At this time, Alicia will continue to deliver ongoing knowledge of her novels with the blessing of her readers. Alicia is also the author of "Diaries of a Dead Woman."

Be on the lookout for Alicia's upcoming projects....

My Poet's Soul
The Epiphany
The Delights of Sin

Visit Alicia online at www.aliciarice.com

Tell Alicia what you think at Alicia@aliciarice.com
She looks forward to your feedback!

www.ingramcontent.com/pod-product-compliance
Lightning Source LLC
Chambersburg PA
CBHW021015180626
46814CB00003B/1302